ADDISON MOORE

Sugar Cookie Slaughter

Murder in the Mix Mystery #18

Edited by Paige Maroney Smith
Cover by Lou Harper, Cover Affairs
Published by Hollis Thatcher Press, LTD.

Books by Addison Moore

Cozy Mystery

Cutie Pies and Deadly Lies (Murder in the Mix 1)

Bobbing for Bodies (Murder in the Mix 2)

Pumpkin Spice Sacrifice (Murder in the Mix 3)

Gingerbread and Deadly Dread (Murder in the Mix 4)

Seven-Layer Slayer (Murder in the Mix 5)

Red Velvet Vengeance (Murder in the Mix 6)

Bloodbaths and Banana Cake (Murder in the Mix 7)

New York Cheesecake Chaos (Murder in the Mix 8)

Lethal Lemon Bars (Murder in the Mix 9)

Macaron Massacre (Murder in the Mix 10)

Wedding Cake Carnage (Murder in the Mix 11)

Donut Disaster (Murder in the Mix 12)

Toxic Apple Turnovers (Murder in the Mix 13)

Killer Cupcakes (Murder in the Mix 14)

Pumpkin Pie Parting (Murder in the Mix 15)

Yule Log Eulogy (Murder in the Mix 16)

Pancake Panic (Murder in the Mix 17)

Sugar Cookie Slaughter (Murder in the Mix 18)

Devil's Food Cake Doom (Murder in the Mix 19)

Mystery

Little Girl Lost

Romantic Suspense
A Sublime Casualty

Romance
Just add Mistletoe

3:AM Kisses (3:AM Kisses 1)
Winter Kisses (3:AM Kisses 2)
Sugar Kisses (3:AM Kisses 3)
Whiskey Kisses (3:AM Kisses 4)
Rock Candy Kisses (3:AM Kisses 5)
Velvet Kisses (3:AM Kisses 6
Wild Kisses (3:AM Kisses 7)
Country Kisses (3:AM Kisses 8)
Forbidden Kisses (3:AM Kisses 9)
Dirty Kisses (3:AM Kisses 10)
Stolen Kisses (3:AM Kisses 11)
Lucky Kisses (3:AM Kisses 12)
Tender Kisses (A 3:AM Kisses Novella)
Revenge Kisses (3:AM Kisses 14)
Red Hot Kisses (3:AM Kisses 15)
Reckless Kisses (3:AM Kisses 16)
Hot Honey Kisses (3:AM Kisses 17)

The Social Experiment (The Social Experiment 1)
Bitter Exes (The Social Experiment 2)
Chemical Attraction (The Social Experiment 3)

Low Down and Dirty (Low Down & Dirty 1)
Dirty Disaster (Low Down & Dirty 2)
Dirty Deeds Low (Down & Dirty 3)

Naughty by Nature

Beautiful Oblivion (Lake Loveless 1)
Beautiful Illusions (Lake Loveless 2)
Beautiful Elixir (Lake Loveless 3)
Beautiful Deception (Lake Loveless 4)

Someone to Love (Someone to Love 1)
Someone Like You (Someone to Love 2)
Someone For Me (Someone to Love 3)

Burning Through Gravity (Burning Through Gravity 1)
A Thousand Starry Nights (Burning Through Gravity 2) Fire
in an Amber Sky (Burning Through Gravity 3)

The Solitude of Passion

Celestra Forever After (Celestra Forever After 1)
The Dragon and the Rose (Celestra Forever After 2)
The Serpentine Butterfly (Celestra Forever After 3)
Crown of Ashes (Celestra Forever After 4)
Throne of Fire (Celestra Forever After 5)

Perfect Love (A Celestra Novella)

Young Adult Romance
Ethereal (Celestra Series Book 1)
Tremble (Celestra Series Book 2)
Burn (Celestra Series Book 3)
Wicked (Celestra Series Book 4)
Vex (Celestra Series Book 5)
Expel (Celestra Series Book 6)
Toxic Part One (Celestra Series Book 7)
Toxic Part Two (Celestra Series Book 8)
Elysian (Celestra Series Book 9)
Ethereal Knights (Celestra Knights)

Season of the Witch (A Celestra Novella)

Ephemeral (The Countenance Trilogy 1)
Evanescent (The Countenance Trilogy 2)
Entropy (The Countenance Trilogy 3)

Melt With You (A Totally '80s Romance)
Tainted Love (A Totally '80s Romance 2)
Hold Me Now (A Totally '80s Romance 3)

1

My name is Lottie Lemon, and I see dead people. Okay, so rarely do I see dead people. Mostly I see furry creatures of the dearly departed variety, aka dead pets, who have come back from the other side to warn me of their previous owner's impending doom. But right about now, I'm not seeing a dead anything. I'm seeing a very angry Lily Swanson who nearly drops a platter of my heart-shaped sugar cookies all over the floor of the community center.

"It's not right." She scoffs as she glares at Naomi Turner, who just so happens to be getting a little too friendly while dripping off of Alex Fox—ex-Marine turned two-timing love machine.

I make a face at Naomi and Alex. It's just the beginning of February, and even though love is in the air, Cupid and his stupid bow seems to be hitting it off the mark already.

"Please ignore them, Lily," I say, pulling her to the left so she doesn't have to see their lust-stricken faces. Lily Swanson is a gorgeous brunette who works for me at my shop, the Cutie Pie Bakery and Cakery. "Besides, it's Naomi's turn to date Alex, not yours." Yes, Naomi and Lily have both agreed to the ridiculous two-timing terms. Since Alex couldn't decide between the two of them, they've been switching off with him every month and it's been a disaster ever since.

Naomi, the other girl in Alex Fox's life, happens to be my best friend Keelie's twin sister. Naomi used to hate me during high school because my then-boyfriend, Bear Fisher, wouldn't cheat on me with her—yes, that's right. And now she continues her disdain for yours truly almost a decade later just because she can. Naomi has dyed her blonde locks a jarring jet-black, and she's a stunner through and through in that shocking pink dress she's squeezed herself into tonight.

Alex Fox is a looker himself—and I should very much think so, considering the fact I'm dating his older look-alike brother, Noah.

Lily groans as we make our way to the extravagant dessert table set out in the middle of the cavernous room. It's the evening of the ribbon cutting ceremony for the renovations taking place, right here at the community center. And seeing that this same establishment is set to host the Vermont's Best Baker competition in just under a month,

Mayor Nash thought it would be a fun idea for all the local bakers to come out and show the fine people of Honey Hollow what they've got to offer. Side note: Mayor Nash hired Bear Fisher, my aforementioned ex-high school not-so sweetheart, to do the renovation.

I spot a couple of my fellow contestants, Whitney Shields and Patricia Engel, laughing it up with a man between them. His arms rest over each of their shoulders, and it looks as if they're having a great time. It seems as if I'm the only baker truly stressed out about the competition.

I wrinkle my nose as I give a glance around at the tired looking structure. "I hope Bear can whip this place into shape in time," I say mostly to myself. My own shop, the Cutie Pie Bakery and Cakery, happens to have a hat in the ring as far as the baking competition is concerned.

"Lottie Kenzie Lemon," a familiar perky voice chirps from behind. "Oh ye of little faith."

I turn to find my best friend, Keelie Nell Turner, with her hands on her hips and a contrived pout on her lips just before she breaks out into a fit of giggles.

"I won't tell Bear you said so." She pulls me in for a quick embrace and I'm momentarily smothered by her blonde curls. Keelie is now engaged to my cheating ex, and basically all of his malfeasances are water under the philandering bridge. Or at least they'd better be. Not only are

Keelie and Bear getting hitched next June, they're expecting a baby next August.

I give her tiny baby bump a gentle pat. "How's my niece or nephew?" Okay, it won't technically be my niece or nephew—but along with the fact that Keelie is my lifelong bestie, we found a little over a year ago that we're cousins, too.

As an infant, I was abandoned at the local firehouse and then quickly adopted by Joseph and Miranda Lemon, but a year ago my birthmother, Carlotta, sprang out of the woodwork and right into my life. Apparently, before she abandoned me, she left a note pinned to the blanket I was swaddled up in and instructed whoever found me to please name me Carlotta. My new mother, Miranda, quickly complied but nicknamed me Lottie right away, and no one has ever called me by my formal name since.

"My baby bear is doing great." Keelie lands her palm lovingly over her tummy. "In fact, the little monster is craving one of your sweet treats." She reaches over and snatches up an adorable heart-shaped cookie iced in pastel pink with the words *you're cute* written on it. I can't help but frown over at the platter of conversation heart cookies.

Lily cackles at the innocent misstep. "That's not Lottie's cookie."

"Nope," a deep voice strums from behind and I turn to find a handsome—okay, *far too handsome* judge who looks as if he's driven here straight from the Ashford Courthouse in his dressed-to-kill dark inky suit.

The judge in question, Essex Everett Baxter, also happens to be my legal husband, but our union is for business purposes only. He basically needed a bride to help preserve his inheritance, and I quickly stepped up to the plate, much to my boyfriend Noah's chagrin.

Yes, that's right. I have a boyfriend *and* a husband, and they're not one and the same.

Everett's lids hood low. "I'd know your cookies anywhere, Lemon." His lips curl in the right direction, but Everett is far too stubborn to ever give a proper smile.

Lemon is the adorable pet name that Everett has had for me for as long as I can remember. And no matter how sour it might sound, I think it's very sweet.

"Get over here, Judge Baxter," I tease as I pull him in for a quick embrace. I'll admit, I steal an extra moment or two locked in his arms just to take in his thick, woodsy cologne. I pull back and get an eyeful of him.

Essex Everett Baxter is a stunner by anyone's definition, with his shock of black hair, those arresting cobalt blue eyes, and a face that looks as if it were chiseled by one of the masters. And don't even get me started on that body. He's slow to smile, quick to leer, and has a surplus of testosterone to outfit a small island nation of men. Every single place he goes, women risk life and limb just to get a better look at him. There is a very good reason the baristas the world over have dubbed him Mr. Sexy. Because it happens to be truth.

Okay, so I might know a little too much about his anatomy, but only because while Noah and I were briefly disrupted in our relationship, Everett and I ended up together—in a very carnal sense.

Noah and Everett were once stepbrothers, and, suffice it to say, they didn't get along. So the fact I was with Everett at all dug open old wounds—wounds that in my opinion have never really healed.

"You look amazing." I shake my head as my eyes ride up and down over him in wonder. Honestly, I shouldn't have said a thing about the way he looks—especially now that Noah and I are giving it another shot—but there's just something exquisite about Everett tonight and I can't quite pinpoint it. His tie flashes silver with a pink patina and his chest is as wide as a linebacker's, but that's not quite it either.

Lily sighs by my side. "She's right, Essex. You look mesmerizing. Now that you're not with Lottie, and it's not my month with Alex—I think you should be my Valentine."

"Oh, hush." Keelie is quick to swat her old friend. "He still belongs to Lottie. Hands off."

My eyes are slow to meet with Everett's, and I cringe.

I clear my throat. "Everett is a free agent." The words are slow to leave my lips, and I regret them as soon as they do.

"Am I?" Everett's chest rumbles with a laugh. "Lemon, the door to your bakery van is still open, and it's snowing outside. Let me know what else you need, and I'll bring it in for you."

"Now that's sweet of you." I bite down on my lower lip and feel my cheeks flush with heat. I'd feel bad for having such a strong biological response to Everett, but it's the same biological response he incites in just about every woman—his mother and sister withstanding.

Even though Everett's first name is Essex, he's always gone by Everett. The only women who call him by his formal moniker are women with whom he's done the mattress mambo. I guess you could say they garner the privilege to use his first name as sort of a door prize—and there are enough women who have garnered the right to call him Essex to fill a football stadium.

Before Everett and I were together, he was a rather prolific playboy. But since we've stalled our relationship—so that I can see where things might lead with Noah—Everett's idea—he hasn't restarted his playboy ways. And if I'm being honest, I'm not too sorry about it either. It feels selfish of me to say so, but I just can't help it.

Lily tightens her coat around her body. "I'll go with you, Essex, and show you what we need."

And yes, Lily has definitely garnered the privilege to call him by his formal moniker.

Everett leans in and dots my cheek with a quick kiss. "I'll be back, Lemon."

The two of them take off, and Keelie is left fanning herself with her fingers as we watch them walk away.

"*Ooh wee!*" She lets out a catcall in his wake, but thankfully there are so many bodies crammed into the community center no one seems to notice Bear's future bride melting at the sight of the good judge. "Is it just me, or has that man turned up the heat?"

"You're not wrong." I snatch the cookie from her hand and take an anxious bite out of it. "Hey? This really is good," I say, looking down at the delectable delight. "But it's not mine. It belongs to Whitney Shields. She's the one that owns the Upper Crust Bake Shop in Fallbrook."

Whitney is a socialite who used to summer with Everett, and seeing that she calls him Essex, they did a little more than relax in the sun together.

Keelie makes a face. "In that case, I'll try to look miserable while eating them."

She glances toward the back of the community center, the same direction Lily and Everett went. I parked the van right next to the kitchen in an effort to traipse through as little snow as possible. It really is coming down out there.

"I don't know, Lot." She shakes her head. "I wouldn't trust Lily Swanson around my boyfriend if he looked like that. Especially since we both know they've been together—and I mean really together."

"I know, I know. But like I said, Everett is a free agent." My heart wrenches again. "I can't stop him from pursuing other avenues while Noah and I feel things out."

"Oh, I get it." She tosses a hand in the air and groans as if arriving at some great epiphany. "It's reverse psychology, Lottie. Of course, he wants you to feel things out with Noah. Once you realize how boring he is, once you compare what the two of them can do underneath the sheets, you'll come to your senses and practically beg the good judge to take you in his chambers."

"*Keelie.*" I can't help but let a husky laugh fly. "Would you stop? Everett is not being manipulative. He can't help how handsome and desirable—okay, fine—and good beneath, over, under, and not anywhere near the sheets he is." I squeeze my eyes shut tight. "And don't you dare tell Noah I said so."

"Don't tell Noah you said what?" Carlotta springs up before us like an unwanted apparition, and I press my hand to my chest with fright.

Carlotta happens to share in my unusual gift to see the dead. We're both transmundane, further classified as supersensual. For some reason or other, I've garnered the ability to see either the ghost of a human or an animal—usually the latter, and at some relatively short span of time

15

after I spot them, something rather gruesome happens to their loved one or previous owner. When I was a kid, it used to amount to nothing more than a sprained knee for the unfortunate recipient, but as of this last year it almost certainly means death. And once the ghost helps me solve their loved one's murder, they up and disappear right back to paradise. Apart from Carlotta, only Noah and Everett know of my morbid abilities.

I make a face at Carlotta without meaning to, because she would definitely tell Noah anything I told her not to tell him. She's not vindictive; she's simply wired that wacky way.

"Never you mind," I say to my older look-alike. Carlotta and I share the same caramel waves and same hazel eyes. I know exactly what I'll look like twenty years down the road if I eschew a good night's sleep and hit the hard liquor every once in a while. "How did it go? Are you all moved in?"

Noah, my handsome, studley, far too kind boyfriend, worked all day so he could help Carlotta move into the spare bedroom of my rental house. Now if that doesn't spell l-o-v-e I don't know what does.

I'm glad to say Noah and I are back on track. We get along great. Heck, his golden retriever, Toby, gets along great with my cats. We're practically one big happy family. It's just that I'm not exactly sure who I should permanently be with when it comes down to Noah or Everett, and I'm utilizing this time with Noah to see if I can gain some clarity on that. You see, when Noah and I had an unexpected breakup, I accidentally fell into the arms of Everett—and Everett very much fell into my heart. It's been complicated ever since.

"You didn't kill him, did you?" I can't help but toss the question her way. Carlotta has been known to be a little rough around the edges, especially where living beings are involved. A thought hits me. "You didn't kick Pancake or Waffles out in this weather, did you?"

Pancake and Waffles are my sweet Himalayan cats. I had Pancake first, then later his brother Waffles was willed to me by my grandma Nell. They're cream-colored balls of fluff with a rust-tipped tail and glowing icy blue eyes.

"Would you relax?" Carlotta snatches up a conversation heart cookie and shoves it into my mouth. "Lighten up. Of course, I didn't kill him. And your cats survived, too. I've still got a few boxes to move, but Harry said he'd help me out tomorrow."

Harry, aka Mayor Nash, was revealed to be my biological father less than a year ago, and I'm still trying to wrap my head around the fact my biological mother and father are dating.

"Great." It comes out depleted and sarcastic, exactly the way I meant it to. The nice thing about Carlotta is that we never have to hide our true feelings from one another, and, oddly enough, feelings never get hurt in the process.

"Don't you *great* me, Lottie Lemon." Carlotta wags a crooked finger at me. "This is all your fault for letting Nell's old place fall to poop."

"What?" I shoot Keelie a look of disbelief and she shrugs over at me. "Carlotta—Bear said he'd get back to me soon with an estimate on repairs. I had no clue Nell's house would need anything done to it. In fact, it was so not *poop* until you started hosting parties with the Canelli girls and turned the living room into a swimming pool." It's true. Last month Carlotta was harboring two Canelli con women in Nell's old house.

I found out about a year ago that Nell Sawyer was my grandmother. Up until Nell died, she was the only one who knew about my supersensual secret. Of course, for a very long time I wasn't even sure what my abilities were called. And when Nell passed away, she left me almost half of Honey Hollow and then some. Let's just say not all of the Sawyers were thrilled with the news, but that's all in the past now. Nevertheless, she left me her old home as well. The very home I'm about to repair, no thanks to Carlotta's costly shenanigans.

Carlotta waves me off and shoves a cookie into her own mouth.

I take another bite of the heart-shaped sugar cookie in my hand and moan without meaning to. "Wow, these really are delicious."

Speaking of delicious—the sea of people parts before me and I spot a deadly handsome, equally wonderful homicide detective with a deep, dimpled grin and eyes the color of the richest evergreen that the great state of Vermont has to offer.

"Noah Corbin Fox." I wrap my arms around him and he gives me a spin before dotting a kiss to my lips. Noah's dark hair is slicked back, his evergreen eyes are pinned heavily on me—and as soon as his dimples depress, every ovary in the room explodes in their honor. Much like Everett, Noah has a way of garnering the attention of every estrogen card-carrying member in the vicinity.

"You look beautiful, Lot." He leans back and inspects me in my fluffy pink sweater, my skintight jeans, and my work boots, which allow me to traipse in and out of the snow without breaking my neck. "Every last inch of you looks delicious." Noah's lids hood as if he were eyeing his favorite meal, and lucky for me I happen to be just that.

"I don't know how I'll ever thank you for helping Carlotta move." I make a face as if I were about to be sick. It's true. I'm not exactly looking forward to having Carlotta as a roommate for the foreseeable future. But with Noah across the street and Everett right next door, that does seem to make things a bit better.

Noah's chest rumbles with a dark laugh. "I have a few ways you can thank me." His brows bounce. "And it was my pleasure. Carlotta surprisingly didn't have many things to move. And we would have gotten it all, but she said she'd do the rest on her own. She didn't want to miss the event here tonight. She wanted to see what you brought to offer for Vermont's Best Baker and so did I."

"Sounds like she got hungry."

"That she did." He glances down at the half-eaten conversation heart cookie in my hand. "That looks amazing."

"That's because it is," says a woman cropping up next to us in a long red dress with her strawberry blonde hair pulled back into a sleek chignon. She's classically pretty with just a simple swath of pink lipstick on her face. It's Whitney Shields, the owner of the Upper Crust Bake Shop, and she's every bit the uppity socialite the name of her bakery suggests.

"Oh, Lottie"—she waves me off with a giggle—"you don't know how much it pleases me to see you eating my cookies." She quickly snatches one up and hands it to Noah. "Go ahead and take a bite. I guarantee you'll fall in love. Just the way you fell in love with Cormack back in high school."

My mouth falls open, but before I can say something, Everett comes back and lands a few platters of my own cookies down on the table.

"Essex." Whitney's arms find a home around him. "How I've missed you." She lands a kiss to his cheek, and suddenly I'm motivated to maim, or kill.

Before Everett can chip her off his side, Cormack Featherby, the aforementioned not-so sweet tart that

20

entranced both Noah and Everett back in high school, pops up like the ghost of girlfriends past. Her shoulder-length blonde hair looks as if she just got a blowout, and her celadon green eyes glow against her porcelain skin. She's wearing a white ruched dress reminiscent of the one I've seen one too many times on the ghost of my good friend, Greer Giles. In fact, it was just a year ago on Valentine's Day that Greer Giles was gunned down. Another far more sinister thought comes to me. Good Lord, she was gunned down right here at the community center.

I scowl over at that white dress Cormack has slinked into as if it were a bad omen of things to come. And considering the girl in the dress, it most certainly is.

"Oh, stop it, Layal," Cormack croaks my way. For reasons unbeknownst to me, Cormack never can get my name straight. "It's all your fault I'm here schlepping gruel instead of dancing with my man." She latches onto Noah like a white dress on rice.

"First"—I carefully peel her off him—"Noah is not your man. He's mine. Noah and I are giving it another shot to see where things end up. Second, it's entirely your fault that you're here whittling down your community service hours. And I highly doubt anyone has you schlepping gruel. But if you need a reminder as to why you're working the room in an entirely blue-collar manner—last month you cat-napped my sweet kitty, Pancake, in an effort to use him as a part of some scheme to break Noah and me up for good."

"And believe me, that breakup is coming." Cormack slaps her palms together in haste as if to say her work here is done.

Right.

Far from it, sister.

"And don't forget Essex." Cormack reaches over and gives the scruff on his cheeks a hasty scratch. "He won't be yours for long either."

"You wish." Keelie leans in as if she's ready to charge.

"Oh, I don't have to wish, Keelie," Cormack is quick to assure her—and with the right moniker. "Once Serena Digby casts a spell on someone, things start to happen. Very bad, bad things."

I can't help but scoff. "Yeah, like money starts to leave your pocket. Newsflash, Cormack: you wasted your time and your spare change."

It's true. Cormack and her featherheaded sidekick, Cressida Bentley, paid some fake enchantress to cast a pox on me. Although I'll admit, for some reason I haven't been able to get Serena's putrid words out of my mind ever since.

You will rue the day you trampled on the hearts of these girls. Everything you love, everything you desire, everything you hope for and dream of will turn to ashes and soot. May nothing go your way. May the shadow replace the sun. May the winds of fortune hide their face from you. May darkness descend on you this hour, and may it never leave until you surrender all that you stole from my sisters.

A shiver runs through me at the thought. "Cormack, in case anyone's never told you—you're nothing but trouble."

Cormack gags and chokes on her next words.

I never stole Noah or Everett from Cormack and Cressida. They're just too smart to want anything to do with those dimwits.

Whitney holds up a hand. "Noah, please call off your girlfriend. She's starting to upset Mack-Mack." She pulls her blonde friend close, and just as she's about to comfort her, she does a double take at something to my right. "Well, if it isn't Pesky Patricia and the Funky Bakery Bunch."

Cormack titters. "Whitney has never cared for Patricia or her friends." She drifts over a few feet before screaming and air kissing a dark-haired woman about the same age before pulling her over. "Everyone, this is Patricia Engel. She owns and runs Patricia's Pastries over in Hollyhock."

"Patricia's Pastries?" Noah inches back. "My mother used to buy all of our birthday cakes from your place."

I can't help but scowl at Noah for a moment with a look that says *traitor*. I know for a fact Patricia's bakery will be my fiercest competition as far as the bake-off goes.

Patricia shrugs it off. Her eyes are heavily drawn in and she's wearing so much foundation it sinks into her laugh lines and the crow's feet starting around her eyes.

"That was my mother's place," she says. "I renamed the bakery when I took over. It's called Sweet Sin now."

Whitney gives a husky chortle. "That's just like you, Patricia. Keeping it classy."

Patricia's lips knot up. "I was keeping it classy right up until you started ripping me off. How dare you flaunt your conversation heart cookies here tonight. You and I both know those cookies are what put me on the map." She turns my way. "I make them year-round and pepper them with fun little political messages. Some of my cookies have been liked and shared thousands of times on social media—by world dignitaries and freedom fighters alike."

"Wow, that's impressive," I say the words apprehensively.

I may not care for Whitney, but I doubt her conversation cookies are anything to write home about—pardon the pun. Not to mention that the fact it was my sister, Lainey, who gave Whitney the idea to make them in the first place. I should know. I was standing right there. And I cringe just a little because I just so happened to have brought my own conversation heart cookies to the ceremony today.

I clear my throat. "You know, Patricia, Valentine's Day is just around the corner and I'm sure you'll see cookies like yours popping up all over the place." Like on those platters I just set down behind her, but I leave that part out.

Patricia rolls her eyes. "But will they say things like this?" She reaches over and swipes up a handful of Whitney's scrumptious cookies—and how I hate that I immediately thought of them as scrumptious—before holding them out for us to read.

Freedom for everyone, this planet is our home, and *justice for all.*

Patricia can hardly catch her breath she's so angry. "These were written on my cookies first. I just love when I give other people good ideas."

Whitney quickly snatches them up. "Don't you dare accuse me of ripping you off. I thought of those slogans all on my own." She quickly stalks off.

Patricia scoffs. "I bet that's right after she saw me posting them to all of my social media sites." She whips out her phone and quickly flashes a picture of one of her posts with cookies that say the exact same thing, written in the same fancy script manner.

Carlotta scuttles over and takes a gander. "I think you've got a case, kid. Have you thought of suing?"

Leave it to Carlotta to invite the legal sharks to the party.

"Nope." Patricia stuffs her phone back into her pocket. "I've thought of murder." She takes off into the crowd herself, and Cormack follows after them.

Carlotta nudges me in the ribs as she snaps up more of Whitney's delectable delights. "I'd keep an eye out for a body if I were you."

"Not funny," I say as Carlotta shuffles her way down the inadvertent bakery aisle we've transformed this place into.

I'm about to say something else when a long glimmer of light glides between the cookie platters like a thick pink and white spotted ribbon of some sort. I lean in, only to have it jump up and nearly bite me on the hand.

A shrill scream evicts from my throat, the kind that's usually reserved for dead bodies—and both Noah and Everett pull me back in an effort to save me.

"What is it, Lemon?"

"Lottie, are you okay?" Noah wraps me in his arms, and yet I only feel a smidge safer.

"There's a snake," I say, pointing right at the beast as it slithers its way down the side of the table before looking right up at me with its dark crimson-colored eyes. It's at least four menacing feet long, and the fact it has playful pink patches all over it doesn't do a lot to comfort me.

"A what?" Everett squints to where I'm pointing. "Noah, do you see anything?"

"No, Everett"—he's slow to answer—"I don't."

"Oh no," I groan.

Noah blows out a breath. "That can only mean one thing."

"Someone is going to die," I whisper. And just like that, the snake up and disappears.

Love might be in the air, but so is murder.

Noah leans in. "Lottie, do you have Ethel with you?" He nods secretly my way. Ethel is the name I gave the gun Noah and Everett teamed up to buy me a few months back. They've both been adamant I keep her with me at all times. And I've mostly complied, with the exception of the bakery. I just hate the thought of bringing something so potentially violent into my sweet, innocent bakeshop.

But the truth is, I don't have Ethel tonight—partly because the day started off at the bakery and will be ending up there as well. And partly because I knew I would have Noah and Everett with me here tonight.

I feel perfectly safe.

Sort of.

I glance to the entry as if anticipating a killer to walk right through it. Instead, I spot an older version of the man who's holding me.

"Oh, Noah," I moan softly. "I think you should take a look at who just walked in."

Both Noah and Everett turn that way and groan in unison at the sight.

It's not the killer, I hope.

It's Noah's father.

2

The community center is thick with bodies, but that doesn't stop Noah, Everett, and me from navigating our way toward the door that Noah's father just walked through. The very same father he believed was dead up until a week ago.

Suffice it to say, Noah's father has terrible timing, considering he's a walking, talking, older version of the man I love, ball of trouble.

Wiley Fox has officially arrived at the community center—yes, *Wiley*.

Everett says that never before has there been a more aptly named individual and Noah agrees with him. Wiley strolled into Honey Hollow and straight into my bakery about a week ago and Noah greeted him by way of gifting him a fist to the eye. Wiley was knocked out cold and bleeding. He even spent a couple of days at Honey Hollow General Hospital, but that was the last we heard of him.

Noah was hoping it would stay that way forever. But, judging by that suit he's donned and that dimpled grin he's shooting the masses, it looks as if Wiley Fox is looking to get comfortable right here in Honey Hollow.

Just as Everett, Noah, and I head on over, I happen to catch a glimpse of Whitney near the kitchen in what looks to be a full-blown argument with a shorter redhead. But the crowd funnels between us, and I miss the socialite sponsored fireworks.

That's too bad. I would have loved to see someone ripping into Whitney. Her entitled attitude, especially when it comes to *Essex*, has really pressed on my very last nerve.

Just before the three of us can get to him, both Carlotta and my mother accost Wiley—and I can't help but note the way my mother is quick to take up his hand and pet it while starting off a conversation with him.

A hard groan comes from me.

Miranda Lemon. Yes, she's the saint that adopted me as an infant. Yes, she had a hard time after my father died and sent her three daughters off to college all on her own. But she's also the same woman who happened to become a bit boy crazy in her golden years.

"*Mother*," I hiss as we come upon them. I make a face at their conjoined hands and she pats him before letting go.

"Hello, gentlemen." Mom offers Noah and Everett a nod.

Carlotta clears her throat. "Wiley here was just telling us that he's got no place to stay." She sniffs over at me as if she wanted me to pipe up with an offer.

Both Carlotta and my mother were with us the day of the big TKO Noah pulled off last week. And rumor has it, my mother visited Wiley in the hospital each day while he was convalescing.

The doctors did every scan under the Vermont sun to make sure he didn't suffer any permanent damage from the fall. Noah was certain that his father would sue him. I can't imagine having a relationship like that with my parents.

I shake my head over at Carlotta. "I can't help him. There's no more room at the inn."

Mom's mouth rounds out as she comes to what I'm sure will be a catastrophic epiphany, and I know so because I can feel it coming a Honey Hollow mile away.

"Wiley, I have an idea." Mom shakes out her blonde curls. Mom has gorgeous vanilla locks and a face that acts as if it has never heard of the term *wrinkles*. She's sassy and a bit too flirtatious for her own good. "I happen to own and operate the Honey Hollow Bed and Breakfast—and I—"

"*No*," both Noah and Everett bark it out in unison.

Noah holds up a hand. "There's no way, no how. That's very kind of you, Miranda, but my father will find some other place to lay his twisted head at night."

Noah might be right about that twisted thing since his father has essentially returned from the dead.

We don't know exactly what happened to sponsor this resurrection, but both Noah and Everett agreed they don't care about the details. Noah wants to push his father into the proverbial grave again, and Everett wants to see the man behind bars.

I guess Noah's father was presumed dead about eight years ago when his boat was found floating in the Pacific without him. I think I kind of get why he would want to disappear. The man has a very dark history with women. He's a classic con artist as far as relationships go. For a brief yet disastrous moment in time, Wiley was married to Everett's mother, Eliza. He bilked her out of some of her fortune before dashing out the door one day and never coming back. And—during that infamous interim, Noah thought it would be a good idea to steal Everett's then-girlfriend Cormack Featherheaded Featherby. Okay, so I threw in that Featherheaded part myself. Nevertheless, suffice it to say, things have never been the same between these two former stepbrothers.

Wiley takes a full breath as he glances to the two men who look prepared to kill him.

"Gentlemen." He nods to Everett first. "How is your mother?"

The muscles in Everett's jaw pop. "Don't you even *think* about my mother. You don't say her name. You don't call, visit, or so much as breathe in her direction."

Wiley's chest expands. "Very well. I will be sure to adhere to your wishes."

Alex crops up with Naomi strapped to his side as if he needed her for protection. Alex is Noah's younger philandering brother, and thus has a deadbeat father of a horse in this race.

"Hey, Pops." Alex takes a moment to frown over at his father. "How are you feeling?"

"Better now." This older version of Noah expands his lips. "And I want to personally thank you for looking after me."

Alex takes a breath. "Yes, well, I didn't have it in me to leave you alone when you had no one else in this world to look after you."

I can feel Noah stiffen with rage by my side.

Alex flashes his brother a momentary smile before reverting to Wiley. "But, now that you're out of the woods, you're on your own. If I were you, I'd scamper right back under that rock you crawled out of."

Mom tosses her hands in the air. "Oh, for heaven's sake. The man just had a traumatic brain injury."

"Actually, that would be his son who suffered a traumatic brain injury. Wiley had a glorified headache," I'm quick to correct. It's true. Just last fall, Cormack wrapped her car around a tree with Noah in the passenger's seat, and everything pretty much went downhill from there. Noah barely survived—*we* barely survived. "And, Mom, I think both you and I should just stay out of this mess."

"Mess is right." Wiley gives a wistful shake of the head. "I was hoping to make amends with my boys—all three of them," he says, looking to Everett. "But I'm not here to take advantage of them in any way."

Carlotta links her arm to his. "Don't you worry, Wiley. If anyone knows what it feels like to have an ungrateful kid, it's me."

"*Hey*," I bleat. "I'm your only kid. Aren't I?"

Carlotta waves me off. "He's moving in with us, Lot. We can't just let this handsome man roam around Honey Hollow, only to find him frozen solid in the morning." She all but nuzzles her face into his neck.

"Carlotta." I make wild eyes at her. "What are you doing? Let go of him." I quickly disconnect the two of them. "I'm sure Mayor Nash wouldn't appreciate this."

"Oh, who the heck cares what Harry appreciates." She turns to my mother. "Word on the street is, he's been stepping out on me."

I grunt without meaning to. "Carlotta, he was stepping out on his wife the first time the two of you tangoed. I hate to say it, but what goes around comes around. We probably should have expected this."

It's true. Mayor Harry Nash is a notorious philanderer.

Carlotta glares at the podium where Mayor Nash is speaking to his constituents.

"I'll give him something to expect." Her upper lip quivers the same way mine does when I'm filled with rage.

Just as I'm about to suggest another option for Wiley, outside of freezing solid, Lily snatches me from the crowd.

"Lottie, they want all the bakers to stand by their desserts. There are reporters here and everything."

"You bet. Excuse me," I say as I leave Noah and Everett to their own destructive devices. I'm not sure what will become of Wiley, but I'm betting it won't be too good.

Lily leads me back to where a group of women all hover around the dessert tables.

"We need to mingle." She takes me by the hand and lands me smack in the middle of a circle of what looks to be bickering bakers.

Lily clears her throat. "Everyone, this is Lottie Lemon. She owns the Cutie Pie Bakery and Cakery and she's going to kick each and every one of your tiny hineys in just a few short weeks."

"*Lily.*" I make a face at her. "I'm sorry," I say to the small group of women. "My assistant is a bit enthusiastic." And obnoxious, but I leave that part out.

Whitney smirks at the thought. "Don't worry, Lottie. She won't be so enthusiastic when it gets down to it. I've never been in a competition that I haven't won."

A dark-haired man steps between us with a lantern jaw, and Whitney's affect brightens at the sight of him.

Whitney leans my way. "Lottie, this is Ian—"

Before she can finish, Crystal Mandrake, my own baking nemesis from Ashford County, lets out an obnoxious bark of a laugh and the man raises his hands as if surrendering and stepping to the side.

Crystal has her dirty blonde hair teased three inches off her head and pulled back into sort of a side ponytail a la ode to the eighties. Her apron is encrusted with hot pink rhinestones that wink out the word *winner* across the front. I remember her wearing one just like it at the bake-off we attended last year—and yes, she ironically won.

Crystal purses her hot pink lips. "And I've never been in a competition that I've lost." She snaps her blonde ponytail my way. "Isn't that right, Lottie?"

"I wouldn't know. I've only been in one competition with you—and yes, you did win that." But only because I was busy saving Everett from a false murder charge. Otherwise, I would have had that in the bag. I think.

Whitney tips her head to the side. "Lottie"—she points to a redhead with sharp features and tight lips, the exact redhead I saw her arguing with earlier—"I, too, have an assistant, Ruthie Beasley. And I'm pretty sure no one is as in tune to one another as Ruthie and me."

Ruthie all but snarls at her, and I have the feeling Ruthie is far more in tune with reality than Whitney is.

Crystal plucks a tall, bony girl from the crowd. "And this is my assistant, Bailey Wade. Nobody assists like Bailey." She gives a little wink to the poor girl. Bailey's face is pasty and pale and she, too, looks a bit too miffed to be here.

Come to think of it, I think grouchy assistants are a running theme.

Crystal smirks my way. "I have Bailey do all of my dirty work."

Lily slaps my back before pulling me in. "You sound just like Lottie."

"Lily"—I step away to get a better look at her—"I do not have you do any dirty work."

Patricia steps forward, her eyes still wild with rage over Whitney's heart-shaped cookie faux pas. "And this is *my* assistant." She slings an arm over a sweet looking girl with crimson hair and bright blue eyes. "Jodie McCloud."

Jodie jerks free. "I'm not anyone's assistant." She averts her eyes. "Patricia here just likes to feel important, isn't that right?" She pokes a finger in her chest, and soon the entire lot of us breaks out into one big argument with our own assistants of all people.

Heaven help us.

Heaven help Lily for accusing me of having her do my dirty work. If dirty work consists of giving her all the hours and cookies she wants, then so be it. I'm guilty as sin.

A pretty brunette steps boldly into our bickering midst, sticks her fingers in her mouth, and whistles like a gym teacher. The entire community center dulls to a quiet hush for a few magical seconds and my ears drink down the much-needed relief.

"My name is Larissa Miller and I'm in charge of all you pecking hens."

I pause to inspect her with her polished navy power suit and silver heels.

She clears her throat. "Now, if you could please stop your clucking for five minutes, I'd love for you to stand by your wares as the city council comes by. It was very kind of them to offer the residents a sample of what you're capable of. Take it from me. When someone gives you a little assistance, you should be grateful."

Her eyes lock with someone behind me and I turn to find both Whitney and Patricia looking a little annoyed by her comment. They're both so entitled, it doesn't surprise me one bit that they can't take a reprimand.

We do as we're told, albeit most of us begrudgingly. Lily is completely acting up today, but every now and again I catch a snippet of Alex striding by with a gorgeous Naomi Turner suctioned to his side like a barnacle and I get it. Of course, Lily is fuming. That would be like me seeing Cormack strapped to Noah's side or Cressida, a horrid socialite who's been after Everett, strapped to his side.

Then, as if the universe were playing some cosmic joke on me—a very bad one might I add—I catch a glimpse of Noah with Cormack attempting to crawl all over him. And Everett with Cressida Bentley gliding up and down him as if he were a stripper pole. Cressida has her pale mane pulled back, her lips are glossy, and there's a laugh bubbling from her—and suddenly I'm ready to spit nails right alongside Lily.

It takes what feels like hours for the city council to sample every cookie, brownie, and pie known to man. Once we're through, I head toward the kitchen with a couple of empty platters that I'm ready to toss into my bakery van, but I stop shy of the entry as I spot Whitney and Patricia going at it.

It looks as if the cookie wars are heating up again. Something tells me this feud will stretch far past Valentine's Day. I bet they'll be sending baskets of cookie hearts to one another with very nasty conversations written on them.

The two of them spot me before Whitney grabs ahold of Patricia and ushers her down the dark hall that leads out to the parking lot.

Just great. As if it wasn't hard enough avoiding their nonsense in a room full of thousands, I'll be forced to walk right past them on the way to my van.

I think on it for a second and head back to the table laden with baked goods and consolidate a few more platters in the name of efficiency. That should give them enough time to kill one another.

I watch as Larissa Miller pulls Crystal Mandrake to the side, and a part of me hopes it's because she wants to disqualify her from the competition altogether. Now that would turn this night around.

That pink slithering snake comes to mind and my eyes spring wide.

Whitney and Patricia just left the building—and they were angry enough to kill.

"Oh my goodness," I whisper as I hustle my way through a thick blanket of people struggling to get back to that dark hall they wandered off in. I can't let Whitney kill Patricia. Actually, I think it was the other way around. Patricia was about to kill Whitney for stealing her cookie— and if they both discovered it was Lainey's idea for Whitney to rip her off, they might team up and kill my sister.

The homicidal possibilities are endless.

I finally navigate my way over, bumping and pushing through a sea of bodies until I hit the hall, but there's a glimmer of light near my feet that steals my attention before I can get to the end of it.

A small fluffy white cat with pale blue eyes sits in front of the darkened hallway and looks up at me with a sweet little meow bleating from it.

"Oh my goodness!" I struggle to balance the trays in my hand. "Aren't you the cutest little thing." I'm about to risk toppling every dish right out of my hands to bend over and pick up the sweet thing just as that pink spotted snake slithers between us. It lifts its head and hisses my way, causing the fluffy little cat to jump on all fours. Its hair rises in every direction at once as if it was just electrocuted, and it bolts right out the back door.

"*Huh.*" I straighten, stunned for a moment. That snake has clearly gone over the rainbow bridge, so how did the cat see it?

Maybe it has a sixth sense or something?

Or maybe it didn't see it at all and it was afraid of me?

Nevertheless, I follow it down the hall and out the door into the dark, snowy night. I step out cautiously, fully expecting that blowout between Whitney and Patricia to still be in full effect, but it's deathly quiet out here and I'm grateful for it.

Not a sign of either one of them.

No sign of a slithering spectral snake, and no sign of that precious white kitty.

Too bad.

I throw my platters into the bakery van and note something moving near the woods just past the parking lot.

I bet it's that cat.

Poor thing will freeze out here if I don't save it.

My feet carry me in that direction, and suddenly I'm wishing I had brought Ethel with me in the event I run into trouble. I'm slow to admit this, but trouble seems to be my middle name.

"Here, kitty, kitty," I sing softly, almost too quiet for any living thing to hear.

The cusp of the forest is about as far as I'm willing to go. I haven't had much luck wandering the woods alone at night. In fact, it usually leads to something nefarious in nature. If I've learned anything, I've learned that the woods and I are not very good friends.

I turn to head back to the community center when to my right I spot what looks like a couple of coats thrown onto the snow and my heart stops cold.

"What the heck?" I whisper as I head that way.

But it's not a couple of coats. It's Whitney Shields and Patricia Engel, lying face up, a platter of my heart-shaped cookies strewn between them—both with a gunshot wound through their chests.

The earth sways beneath my feet, and a scream gets locked in my throat.

My goodness. They're both dead.

I spin on my heels to get help just in time to see a long, dark board coming down over my head and the world goes black.

3

My head hurts.

A hearty moan rips from my throat.

"Lottie?" A male voice sounds as if it's coming in and out. "*Lottie*," he riots hard over my face as my lids slowly flutter open. "There you go. She's coming to, Everett."

"Noah," I mumble as I blink to life. "Everett?" The world comes into focus, and I see Noah's worried face hovering over mine. "*Noah*."

"I'm right here." He dots a soft kiss to my lips.

Everett lands his jacket over me and immediately I'm covered in his warmth and the spiced scent of his cologne.

It takes everything in me to sit up. "What happened?" No sooner do the words tumble out of me than I spot a couple of bodies lying in the snow next to me and it all comes rushing back. "Noah, they're dead, aren't they? Oh my word."

I struggle to inch my way away from them as my head ricochets with pain.

"Whoa, Lemon." Everett is quick to kneel to my right and block the morbid view.

"Is it true?" I nod to him and Noah. "Whitney and Patricia are gone?"

Noah's dimples dig in. "Yes, Lottie. They are."

The howl of a siren pierces the night, and Noah reaches for his gun.

"Lottie, what did you see?" he pants. "Who did this to you?"

A spark of light goes off in the woods, and I squint into the night, trying to make out any ghostly companions that might be lurking nearby.

"There was a cat—and a snake." I point to the woods. "I was trying to save the cat from freezing to death, but I couldn't find it. Instead, I found..." I can't seem to find the words to finish the morbid sentence.

Noah glances up at Everett. "Okay, I'm going to comb the woods. Whoever did this might still be out there. See if you can get her out of the snow. I want her checked out by a medic. Do *not* leave her alone. You got that?" He presses a kiss to my cheek before drawing his weapon and speeding for the woods.

In a moment the place is crawling with sheriff's deputies and firemen. And before Everett helps me to my feet, the coroner's van pulls up.

Forest Donovan runs up in his turnout gear. His boyish face is filled with worry as he claps his hand over my shoulder. "Lottie, what the hell happened?"

Forest is my brand new brother-in-law as of last year. He and my sister, Lainey, are expecting a baby this August and I couldn't be happier for them.

"I don't know. I found Whitney and Patricia lying in the snow, and then someone came out of the blue and whacked me on the head."

"You were hit?" His eyes fill with anger. "Everett, get her inside. I'll send a couple of EMTs to check her out." He shakes his head at Everett. "Can't believe we've got a double homicide on our hands."

"Double homicide?" My fingers float to my lips. "Oh my goodness, things aren't getting better. They're getting worse."

That curse Serena Digby threw my way last month comes back to me, and suddenly I feel remotely responsible for the double trouble that's befallen this sweet town.

"Did I hear double homicide?" a female voice trills to my right and we turn to find Noah's partner, Detective Ivy Fairbanks, with her dark hair pulled back. Her pale features look a little too sculpted as the moon shines over her. Ivy is beautiful, and for a very long time I've suspected she's had a little crush on Noah. But when it comes to me, she can be downright nasty.

She smirks my way. "Lottie Lemon. Why aren't I surprised to see you at the nexus of all this criminal activity?" She openly snarls at me. "I wouldn't leave town if I were you."

Everett and I watch as she stalks off to the scene of the crime.

"Come on, Lemon." He carefully navigates me to the entry. "Let's get you a seat, and I'll make sure you have something warm to drink. How does your head feel?"

"Horrible. It's throbbing, and it feels as if the world is throbbing right along with it."

"I'm going to kill whoever did this."

I glance up at him in horror. Sadly, I know he's not kidding. Everett really would kill to keep me safe.

Soon, we're right back in the heart of the community center with the hustle and bustle of bodies circulating through the room, oblivious to the evil that just took place outside, and Everett lands me in the first chair he finds.

"Lottie!" Lainey trots over, waddling a bit more than usual due to the growing size of her adorably tiny belly. Lainey and I share the same caramel-colored hair and hazel eyes. I used to think that my parents were mistaken about my adoption because Lainey and I looked so much alike, but they never changed their story. "Is it true? Forest just texted and said you found two dead bodies!"

As much as I want to press my finger to my lips and shush her, I can't help but groan instead. The throbbing in my head seems to be pulsating along with the laughter and din of conversation around us.

Our sister, Meg, blinks to life beside her.

"Of course, it's true." Meg barks out a laugh. Meg has dyed her blonde locks jet-black and it looks stunning juxtaposed against her icy blue eyes. She worked for years in Las Vegas on the female wrestling circuit but has been back in Honey Hollow for a while now teaching strippers their sultry moves down in Leeds. "Lot knows where all the bodies are buried. Or should I say dropping dead? I guess they're not buried yet, are they?" She chuckles.

"*Meg,*" I reprimand, and a spear of pain ignites at my temples. "We'd better keep it down. I'm pretty sure they have friends in this room that still don't know what's going on."

Lainey sucks in a quick breath. "So there *were* two people who were killed!"

A round of gasps circles through the crowd, and soon the room breaks out into whispers.

"Perfect," I say. "Way to cause mass hysteria. Now everyone will know that Whitney and Patricia were gunned down."

"Whitney and Patricia?" a sharp cry of a female rings out their names, and I cringe.

Okay, so I don't do my best thinking after I've been bopped on the head.

I turn to find Jodie McCloud with her hand pressed to her chest, and soon enough all the bakers and their ornery assistants to boot have huddled around her, clamoring for details no one quite has.

Mom ambles up with Wiley Fox by her side, and I can't help but scowl. Good Lord help us all if he makes a play for my mother. On second thought, it's Wiley who will need all the help he can get. There's no way I'll stand by and watch as someone tries to take advantage of my mother.

"Oh, Lottie." Mom throws herself over me as she offers up a firm embrace. "Tell me you're all right. Mayor Nash was just outside, and he said there was a murder. He said something about you being hurt. Are you okay?"

"I'm fine." I lean back and the room sways.

Wiley leans in and inspects both of my eyes, and I would swear on all that is holy that it's Noah looking at me with love. They share the same evergreen eyes, the same deep-welled dimples, same just about everything.

Oh, it's no use. If this man sets his *wily* sights on Miranda Lemon, my mother is toast.

"Where's Noah?" he says it softly—and oddly, he not only looks like his oldest son, he sounds like him, too.

Everett gives the man a shove and sends him stumbling back.

"You don't get to talk to her. If you want Noah, head out in the woods and find him yourself."

"Don't go out there, Wiley," I'm quick to tell him. "There's a killer on the loose. It's dangerous out there. Noah has a weapon. He's a trained professional. He'll be fine."

Everett growls at the older man, "If you want to be of help, go out and find a medic and get them inside. She was hit on the head. She needs medical attention."

"Oh dear." Mom takes off her coat and tucks it around me like a blanket just as Forest heads this way with a couple of beefy men carrying enough medical equipment to outfit a hospital.

Lainey heads over. "Forest is here, and he's brought help," she shouts so loud her voice goes off like a gong in my head.

Meg steps between us. "She's not hard of hearing, Lainey. Why don't you go grab her a cup of hot java? I think Lottie needs a good jolt. She looks as if she's about to pass out."

"Good thinking." Lainey trots off just as Carlotta and Mayor Nash scuttle over.

"Oh my Honey Hollow stars," Carlotta bleats. "They've done killed our baby!"

"Carlotta," I hiss. "I'm not dead." I crimp my lips at her.

Mayor Nash leans in so close I can see my reflection in his eyes.

"Nope." He shakes his head. "She's still kicking. That's my girl." He offers up a firm slap to my shoulder, and I bite down on my lip to keep from yelping. Heaven knows Everett would drive me straight to the hospital himself if he knew how terrible I really felt.

The medics check me out, and sure enough they suggest I get some rest—but only if someone watches me, lest something goes deadly wrong in my sleep.

Carlotta straightens. "I'll keep an eye on ya, kid. Good thing I moved in when I did. I'll make sure to do a room check every fifteen minutes just like they do on the psych ward."

All the commotion around us stops briefly as we all steal a moment to gawk her way.

I'd ask how she was privy to the rules of a psych ward, but I'm half-afraid she'll answer.

"No," Everett says, his eyes still very much locked over mine. "I'm staying the night. Noah will be gone for hours. I'm taking care of you, Lemon. I'll make sure you're okay."

A choir of audible sighs circle behind him and I crane my neck to see Lily, Naomi, and Alex.

Soon enough, Mayor Nash announces that it's safe for everyone to vacate the premises, and the room begins to slowly drain of bodies.

The medics leave, and Everett helps me to my feet.

Mom offers me a tender kiss on the cheek before turning his way.

"Judge Baxter, I can't thank you enough for looking after my baby girl. Should she need anything at all, Carlotta will be in the very next room."

My mouth falls open and she twitches a guilty smile.

"Fine. Call me instead." She glances over to Wiley as Carlotta does her best to paw at him in a cheap attempt to rile up Mayor Nash—and how I hope that's all it is.

The last thing I need is both Carlotta and my mother vying for his criminal affection. And believe me, that alone would be criminal in so many ways.

Mom gurgles as she gazes at him. "But if I'm lucky, I might have company." She clip-clops over to him and I try to lunge after her, but Everett catches me in his strong, thick arms and soon I can feel the pounding of his heart beating over mine.

"Don't you worry, Lemon. I'm going to squash this like a bug."

Carlotta comes up and Everett leans me up against her.

"I'll be right back, Lemon."

Everett takes off to where my mother is busy accosting Noah's look-alike, and it feels downright wrong to see her doing it.

Carlotta points down abruptly. "Well, lookie here, Lot Lot. We've got visitors."

I glance down in time to see her picking up one of the cutest fluffy white cats you ever did see. She has a glowing aura about her, a pink patina with a touch of iridescent baby blue around her face, and her fur looks as if it's managed to trap an entire constellation of stars.

"Hello there," I say, lightly scratching my finger over the top of her magical little head. "What's your name, sweetie?"

Not that long ago, my supernatural abilities grew. At first, I couldn't hear the dead at all, but slowly as my powers began to flourish so did their abilities. The dead were able to move things in the material world, a horror if ever there was one. Then the dead garnered the ability to speak, and thankfully so. It's so much easier to get their points across now. And just a couple of months ago, they acquired the very best ability of all—at least according to them—they can *eat*.

"*Princess*," the tiny creature purrs it out low and sultry with a heavy emphasis on the rolling of the R. "And why is it I'm back here? Where is my sweet girl?" She blinks her long thick lashes at the room as if she were still trying to get her bearings.

Before I can open my mouth to reply, the most frightening phantasm of them all, that pink and white spotted snake slithers its way up through the air and I can't help but take a full step back in its presence. Dead or not, it's a menacing sight.

"You're back because she's dead, dumb dumb," the snake warbles it out in a deep baritone before bopping its pink spotted tail on the tiny cat's head.

"*Ha!*" Carlotta balks at the sight of the floating serpent. "You're a boy, aren't you? Typical man trying to put a woman down. Apologize to her or I'll have your revenant rights revoked."

The sinister snake doesn't hesitate to hiss right at her.

"Yes, genius. I'm a boy." He snaps his head my way. "I've heard rumors of whiskey. Is this true?"

Carlotta smacks me on the arm. "That reindeer we had a couple months back must be spreading the word." She leans close to the spotted spirit. "I think you and I are going to get along just fine. What's your name, handsome?"

His mouth pulls down, and if I didn't know better, I'd think he was frowning.

"Taffy."

"*Taffy?*" Carlotta and I belt it out in unison.

Carlotta shakes her head. "Let me guess. Princess here belonged to Miss Goody Two-Shoes, and Laughy Taffy was doling out constricting hugs to good old sinful Patricia."

"That I was." Taffy gives a dark chortling laugh. "I think I like you." He slithers his way around Carlotta's shoulders just as Everett comes back.

"All right, Lemon." He wraps an arm around me. "It's time to hit the sheets."

Another round of sighs break out around us as a group of women stride by.

Carlotta gives a wistful shake of the head. "If I had a dime every time I've heard a man say that to me."

Taffy rumbles another dark laugh. "I had a hunch you were a naughty one."

Carlotta knocks her head to his. "And I have a hunch you were no slacker yourself with the ladies."

Everett leans in. "Who's she talking to?"

"A snake," I say as I shrug up at him. "Quick, take my hand." About a year ago, we discovered that I act as a conduit, and if someone happens to be holding my hand at the right time, they can hear the dead speak, too. "And in my arms is the prettiest little kitty you ever could meet. If my fur boys could see her, they would just eat her up. She's just that sweet."

"Did you say *boys*?" Princess perks to attention at the mention of the male species. "I do love me some men." She lets out a rollicking purr, and both Everett and I share a warm laugh.

"Lucky for you," I say. "I've got two of them." I meant cats, but Everett gives me a wink as if acknowledging this in an entirely different way.

Outside, the parking lot is quickly emptying as one car after the other speeds off toward Main Street.

But something down at the other end of the lot snags my attention.

"Everett, look," I whisper, and he follows my gaze as we watch as a familiar looking redheaded woman gives a man in a suit a hard shove to the chest. He has dark hair. His limbs look lanky as he towers over her.

"I'll keep an eye on things in case it gets ugly, but let's get you to the car. Lily said she's taking your van back to the bakery."

But I don't move. I watch as the man seems to grow more animated before he takes off and jumps into his own car.

Everett sighs as it wraps up. "What do you think that was about?"

"I don't know," I say. "But I'm pretty sure the woman was Jodie McCloud."

"I guess I know who we'll be questioning first."

"We?" I bite down on my lip as I look up at him, doing my best to suppress a smile.

"That's right, Lemon. It looks like we're back in business."

It's February.

Love is in the air.

And so is murder.

4

Everett didn't take me home.

Not right away at least. He drove me straight to Honey Hollow General and had my head examined—literally. They ran every test, scan, and eye exam known to man before sending us on our merry little way with a clean bill of health.

True to his word, Everett watched over me as I fell asleep. And when I woke up, I was already back in Noah's arms.

But at the moment I'm at the Cutie Pie Bakery and Cakery, and the morning rush has just died down. I spent all morning losing myself in my baking, and now the shelves are filled with fresh raspberry Danishes, chocolate éclairs, classic peanut butter cookies, lemon bars, and blueberry almond shortbread.

I pat Princess on the top of her soft fluffy head absentmindedly. How I wish I could bring Pancake and Waffles to the bakery. Now that would be a *purrfect* day.

Outside, the snow is falling steadily as I take in the butter yellow walls of the bakery and the pastel mix and match furniture scattered about the seating area. They say there's no place like home, and, lucky for me, I really do have two of them.

The bakery is my baby through and through. Before Nell died and willed the place to me, she had a walk-through put in between the shared wall of the bakery and the Honey Pot Diner next door.

The Honey Pot was Nell's baby. It's been a fixture here in Honey Hollow for over fifty years. There's a large resin oak tree in the middle of it whose branches extend over the ceiling and straight into the café portion of my bakery. Each branch is lovingly wrapped in twinkle lights and it gives off a magical appeal.

Lily slings a kitchen towel over her shoulder. "Thank goodness you made a surplus of your iced sugar cookies. Can you believe both of those girls each had one in hand when they bit the big one? Hey? I bet our sales double, too!"

I cringe at the morbid thought. It's true. For some unknown reason, the recent string of homicide victims all seemed to be noshing on one of my sweet treats when they met their demise.

Lily yawns as we enjoy the lull. "I didn't catch a wink of sleep last night."

Princess arches her back and yawns herself. "Neither did I. Those boys of yours ignored me, Lottie. I've never been more affronted in my entire charm-filled life." She shakes out her fur and sparks fly from her.

I wrinkle my nose at Princess before turning to Lily. "Is it because you were afraid there was a killer out there and they were going to get you?"

"No." She checks her reflection in the glass bakery shelves and frowns. "Because I knew Naomi was going home with Alex."

"Ugh. He's such a pig. I'm sorry, Lily. But what's fair is fair. If he gets to have someone else every other month, so should you."

She gasps at the thought. "And cheat on Alex for six months out of the year? But what if I lose him?"

"Then he was never yours to begin with. And don't you start comparing this to Noah, Everett, and me. We don't switch off-months."

"I know, Lottie. You're not that lucky."

"Or that deranged."

My mind drifts a moment as I start to envision what that arrangement might be like. Noah and me. Everett and me. Noah and—

"Go ahead and say it." Lily folds her arms over her chest. "I know you're thinking it. One long luscious month in Noah's arms—then four hot, steamy weeks doing unimaginable things with Essex."

I'm practically drooling right up until she calls Everett by his proper moniker.

"Would you stop calling him that? It makes my mind bend in all sorts of twisted directions. And believe me, the last thing I want to envision is you with Everett."

A dull laugh bounces from her. "Why not? He's available, isn't he?" She bats her lashes at me in an obnoxious manner.

"No," I flatline. "He's off limits."

Princess lets out a sharp meow as if agreeing with me. "You tell her, Lottie." She shakes out her fur and sparkles with stardust. "A girl can never have too many men in her life."

I twist my lips at that one. I'm pretty sure it's entirely untrue, but a part of me happens to agree with her. Especially if the men are Noah and Everett.

The bell on the door chimes and in strides a small army of sweaty women with winter coats thrown over their yoga gear, their hair in slightly disheveled ponytails, and each of their faces is a matching slapped-cheek red.

Britney makes her way over with her long strawberry blonde ponytail swinging, save for one loose strand that cleverly hides her left eye.

Britney Fox—as in Noah's first ex-wife—myself accidentally being the second—lands her hands on the counter as if she were about to make a demand.

"Whatever you did to those blonde bimbos, undo it," Britney spits it out as if she were fighting mad.

Britney is a sultry, human version of Jessica Rabbit, with her perfect curves and full ruby red lips. The two of us didn't quite get along in the beginning, but we seem to be on the same page as of late about a lot of things.

"What are you talking about? What bimbos?" I crane my neck into the crowd, but I don't see a sign of anyone I know.

Britney scowls. "They're coming in hot, right behind me. Just know I don't appreciate any black magic shenanigans going on in my gym."

Britney owns and operates several Swift Cycle gyms sprinkled around Vermont. One of which happens to be right across the street from my bakery. And when class lets out, she promptly walks them right over to have a nice cup of coffee and a little sweet treat. That way they put back all the calories they spent the last sixty minutes cycling off. It's a win-win for both Britney and me.

I suck in a quick breath as the two blonde bimbos walk into the bakery.

"You mean Cormack and Cressida? They brought their friend to the gym?"

Britney averts her gaze. "If by 'friend' you mean friendly neighborhood sorcerer, you'd be right. She had the whole class chanting, casting who knows what kind of a pox by the end of the hour. And when I asked them to stop, they said they couldn't. The head wizard said something about needing to keep the momentum going. She even went as far as to imply that you would be the next dead baker."

Both Lily and I gasp at that one.

Princess lets out a yowl before prancing on over. "What is this melee? Are you going to die, too, Lottie?"

"I'm not going to die." I shake my head empathically just as the wicked trio—Cormack, Cressida, and a sweaty Serena Digby—stride on over, each with a gloating grin.

Cormack leans in; her pert little nose is slightly turned up. "Just so you know, the Big Boss called and he's invited me over for dinner."

I gulp audibly at the thought.

"Noah invited you to dinner?" I tip my head her way as if I didn't hear her right.

"Yup. I'll be by at six. Noah and I would appreciate our privacy. Maybe you could skedaddle on over and pay Essex a little visit in his private chambers? Rumor has it, the naughty judge is feeling left out in the cold these days."

Cressida elbows Cormack hard in the ribs. "Mackie, he's mine, remember? You can't just take Noah and run. We hired Serena to seal the deal for the both of us."

"*Hired?*" I smirk over at the dark-haired witch with the face of an angel. "Some friend you turned out to be. I'll have you know my bestie would cast a spell for free if she could."

Serena's eerie smile widens as it stretches over half her face. "Believe me, if you knew what the future had in store, you would be throwing fistfuls of dollars my way just to reverse the curse."

Lily leans in. "You can reverse the curse?"

"Sure I can." Serena lifts a shoulder our way as if she were flirting. "For a *fee*."

I smack my hand over the counter just the way Brit did when she arrived.

"Knew it," I say. "It's a scam. The three of you are baiting me to turn over my life savings out of fear. Well, I'm not doing it."

Lily cocks her head at the girl. "You wouldn't happen to have a love potion, would you?"

My mother pops up from behind them, and I jump at the sight of her.

"Did someone say love potion?" Mom giggles while patting her lips with her fingers. "I'll take two, please."

I wave my mother to the side, happy to leave the tall, gaunt, and haunted trio to their own wicked devices.

I glance back to the register. "And no love potion for you, Lily. We want true love. Not a bottle of tequila with a wicked worm in it."

Cormack leans my way. "You'll never have Noah."

Cressida shakes her head. "Essex is mine."

I raise a brow at Serena. "What have you got?"

She bats her lashes at me before glancing around the bakery, and her face falls flat.

"I sense evil." No sooner does Serena hiss the words out than poor Princess arches her back and lets out a hair-raising cry before disappearing altogether.

Believe you me, there are plenty of moments in my life where I wish I had that superpower. And right now is one of them.

I offer my full attention to my mother while Lily whispers to Serena.

"What can I help you with, Mom? A scone? A pink thumbprint with sprinkles? Raspberry Linzer hearts? Cherry tarts? Jelly roll to go?"

"Ooh, it all sounds so delicious, but I'm afraid I'm going to have to watch my waistline. Just a few chocolate filled croissants will do." She gives a sly wink.

"So, how did it go with Wiley last night?" I make a face as I quickly put her order together and throw in a few raspberry Linzer cookies as well for the heck of it.

She frowns at the mention of his name, and that sight alone makes me happy.

"It didn't go anywhere," she pouts. "Can you believe that man rebuffed me? And he refused to stay at the B&B. Something about keeping his nose in place."

"Sounds like Everett's threats really worked."

"Oh, you kids," she hisses. "I wish you'd leave me to my own devices."

"We're petrified of your own devices. We've seen where they lead you. Does the Jungle Room in Red Satin ring a bell?"

Red Satin happens to be the gentlemen's club where Meg teaches strippers their night moves. And the Jungle Room is a kinky convention center in their basement where all kinds of illegal and lascivious things come to pass. It's no place for a mother, especially not mine. And sadly, her dicey boyfriends have dragged her there on more than one occasion.

"Well, don't you worry." Her upper lip twitches. "Chrissy Nash and I have decided we're going to take the month dedicated to love by the horny horns and partake in every salacious adventure the next few steamy dreamy weeks have to offer." Her shoulders shimmy in a way that lets me know naughty things are afoot.

"Lovely," I say, pushing a hot coffee her way. "I won't have to worry about you one bit." I'll have to worry about her a *whole lot*.

"Of course, I'll be hosting a few of those soirees myself. The matchmaker mixer, the truth or dare affair, and the Valentine's salacious scavenger hunt." She nods as if it were business as usual. "In fact, the matchmaker mixer is coming up in just a few days, and I really need you to step up to the cookie plate and deliver the goods. Oh, and there's a book club meeting tomorrow at the B&B, and I wanted to know if I could order a few platters for that as well."

"Sure thing. I'll bring them by myself."

"Perfect. We're meeting at two." She gives a quick wave as she heads for the door. "I need to get my hair touched up. I've invited Wiley to the book club!"

Great. Wiley Fox trapped in a room full of women of a certain age. It really will be like letting a fox loose in a henhouse.

A thought comes to me and I look to Lily. The counter has cleared of customers, and she's back to staring vacantly out the window.

"Do me a favor and call the Sweet Sin Bakery over in Hollyhock, would you? Ask them to bring over three platters of their best cookies to my mother's B&B tomorrow at two."

Lily gives a few solid blinks. "But you just told her you'd cater the event."

"And I most certainly will. But if I'm lucky, Jodie will deliver the platters herself."

"*Ah*"—Lily tips her head back—"and then you can question a suspect."

"Now you're catching on."

Lily squints at something behind me. "What's that?"

I turn to find a small black gift bag on the counter.

"Did anyone leave a bag here?" I hold it up, and a few people shake their heads before returning to their conversations.

"Lottie, look." Lily turns a small tag over. "It says your name."

"Lottie Lemon," I read. "That it does."

I pull the little black bag close and pull out a wad of black tissue paper. It's lighter than air, and I unfurl it with the utmost care.

"What is it, Lottie?" Lily tugs at my sleeve. "Well, what is it?"

I pull back the last bit of tissue paper, exposing a heart-shaped cookie burnt to a crisp. Black icing covers the front, and there's just one simple word on it.

Die.

5

My mother's bed and breakfast has always reminded me of a Gothic haunted mansion with its enormous pale exterior. And interesting to note—it's actually haunted.

No sooner do Keelie and I load ourselves up with cookie platters than a rather fancy sedan pulls alongside us and a drop-dead gorgeous judge from Ashford County jumps out looking fit to kill.

I stagger under the heft of my sweet treats, trying not to slip in the snow. I've got red velvet cupcakes with decadent cream cheese frosting, sweetheart mini cupcakes—a vanilla cake filled with strawberry cream, chocolate chip cookies, frosted fudge brownies, blondie bars, cocoa powder truffles, and, of course, a huge assortment of my iced conversation heart-shaped sugar cookies. Princess helped me think up all sorts of cute little sayings to write on them. She really is a natural when it comes to amorous affection.

"Everett?" I call out as he dashes past me.

"I'll see you inside, Lemon." He darts off like a man on a mission and Keelie and I exchange a quick glance before hightailing it right in after him.

Inside, it's as warm as a hug with the dark wooded wainscoting and the thick lush carpeting that dampens the sounds of our frantic footsteps.

"He's headed for the conservatory," I say to Keelie as we amble our way in that direction.

Last night, Noah came home late, and by the time we had dinner and dessert—dessert might have led to other far more delicious things—well, I didn't tell Noah or Everett about the cookie of death I received at the bakery. All in due time, I suppose, and something tells me that due to the emergency Everett seems to be having, this won't be the right time either.

The lobby of the B&B is sparse with guests, most of which are women of a certain age, all streaming to the right where my mother has an enormous sitting room. I glance over to see a roaring fire already underway and my mother speaking to the women gathering for her mostly naughty book club.

An illuminated being crops up and floats alongside me, and it just so happens to be the ghost of Greer Giles. Greer is a girl about my age who was shot in the chest last winter. She's a gorgeous brunette who could win any ghostly beauty pageant that the other side has to offer. Her vellum-like body glitters with sparks of light, and her dark hair looks as if she's accessorized it with stars.

"Guess what, Lot?" She flashes a ghostly smile my way.

I hitch my head toward Keelie and shake it. There's no way I'm having a conversation with the dead in front of my bestie. Not only is she not apprised of my ability to see the deceased, but I'd hate to make her question my sanity while she's in such a delicate state. The safety of Keelie's baby is of the utmost importance to me.

Greer rolls her translucent eyes. "Fine. I'll do all the talking. My dead day is coming up and I was hoping you'd bake me a cake. My favorite—"

"Your dead day?" I blurt without meaning to, and Keelie offers me a knowing nod.

Keelie pauses as she cranes her neck into the conservatory. "I see him, too, Lot. But I wouldn't go threatening to kill him. He's already on everyone's hit list. Face it, just having you in the vicinity is enough to do the dirty deed."

"What are you talking about?" I peer and a horrific moan comes from me once I spot the manipulating malfeasance.

Wiley Fox is chest to chest with Everett while Eliza and Suze stand to the side with their jaws rooted to the floor.

I suck in a quick breath. "I think I know why Everett looked as if he were about to send someone straight into eternity—because he was."

Greer gives a haunted moan. "Oh, go on, Lottie. We'll finish up the details of my dead day later."

Keelie and I put the platters down in haste as we make our way over.

I quickly sandwich myself between the two gorilla chested men and expand their distance with my arms. "Whatever's happening, make it stop."

Eliza gives a dark laugh.

Eliza Baxter, Everett's mother, shares her son's inky dark hair and cobalt blue eyes. She's a socialite from Fallbrook who inherited a huge hotel fortune from her father.

I've always liked Eliza and I'd like to believe we get along just fine.

The feisty blonde next to her with short hair that swoops to the side a la boy bands of the nineties—well, she and I are a different story. Suze Fox, yes, the very woman who birthed Noah, is fiery and obnoxious, mean and all around angry at the world. She'd rather shoot me than hug me. But from what I hear, that's par for the course with her.

Eliza quickly plucks me from their masculine midst. "Come now, Lottie. I'd like to see Essex blow a hole through that wily Fox's skull just the way he promised." Both Eliza and Everett's sister call Everett by his proper moniker because it's the only name they've ever called him.

A growl works its way up my throat. "Don't you dare, Everett. He'll sue you and probably get you disbarred and thrown off the bench for good. It's not worth risking all you've worked for."

Suze grunts, "My son knocked him out cold and nearly killed him last week." She bleeds a black smile. "Personally, I was rooting for death."

Eliza's mouth falls open. "Essex, this man has been in town for seven days and you've neglected to warn me properly?"

Everett lowers his chin, his eyes red with rage. "Only because I knew you'd put a hit out on him. I was preparing to ease you into the news."

Eliza's lips twist to the side. "You're right about the hit." She steps in and pokes her finger against Wiley's chest, and this older version of Noah picks up her hand and kisses the back of it in one svelte move.

"My beautiful Eliza. Can you ever forgive me?"

"*No*," Everett and I sing out in unison.

Keelie gives me a quick tug. "I think that girl from Sweet Sin is here. Someone just walked by carrying a platter of cookies."

"Oh, I hope that's Jodie," I say. "Head to the kitchen and stall her. I'll be there in a second."

Eliza draws her hand back. "Why should I forgive you?" she bellows at Wiley. "Why aren't you dead? And more importantly, where is my money?"

Suze squints as she points a crooked finger my way. "I'll tell you where it is. My son put it in her bakery."

My hand flies to my lips.

It's true.

Noah said he wanted the money he received from his father's will to go to something good. He said he tried to give Eliza her money back, but she refused. So he gave it to me and I ended up buying all the appliances I'd needed to start my bakery.

Eliza waves it off. "Don't you worry, Lottie. I don't want anything from you other than grandchildren."

I cringe because I'm not all certain that Eliza realizes Everett and I are married in name alone. And according to the terms of that inheritance of his, that we were trying to preserve, we need to remain legally matrimonially bound until next Christmas.

"And on that note"—I shrug up at Everett—"I think I'd better head to the kitchen. Don't you dare leave without saying goodbye to me."

Eliza twitches her brows. "Better yet, why don't the two of you get a room? If you get busy, I could be holding a Baxter bundle of joy by Christmas."

Everett's lids hood low as if he were game—at least for the getting the room part. And like it or not, my stomach bisects with heat at the thought.

I make a mad dash out of the conservatory before I end up with a baby Baxter to call my own.

I have no doubt Everett and I would have beautiful babies that would grow up to rule over the land in the legal sense or bake up a storm and truly become the best bakers of Vermont, but it's not something I'm striving for at the moment.

Greer finds me in the lobby and zooms up with her three ghostly counterparts. The first is her boyfriend, a handsome farmer with dirty blond hair and a crooked grin who happened to have died over two hundred years ago right here in Honey Hollow, Winslow Decker. The second is a little girl with long stringy hair that covers her adorable face. She wears a dirty pinafore and scuffed Mary Jane slippers, and let's not forget the machete swinging from her wrist. Her name is Azalea, better known as Lea. And last but not least, a friendly black cat whose fur sparks with onyx stars named Thirteen.

While my mother doesn't personally know the ghosts that haunt her B&B, she's grateful to them on so many levels.

A while back her B&B was hardly making ends meet, but once Greer and the gang turned up the spooky heat, my mother was wise enough to capitalize off it in what she's dubbed The Haunted Honey Hollow B&B Tour. She runs tours through the facility at eighty bucks a pop. And once she's done scaring the socks off of people, she sends them straight to the Cutie Pie Bakery and Cakery for what she's dubbed as The Last Thing They Ate Tour—in which the tourists buy out whatever morbid dessert the latest homicide victim in town was found munching on when they met their demise. Suffice it to say, my conversation heart-shaped cookies have really been a hit.

"Lottie, is it true?" Lea wields her weapon before me like a threat and stops me in my tracks. "Has there been a slaughter of plenty?"

"If by 'slaughter of plenty' you mean a double homicide, the answer is yes. It was terrible. And the killer almost got me, too."

The four of them gasp.

Winslow leans in. "That explains the troublesome twosome in the kitchen. They've been wreaking havoc on the pantry."

Greer nods. "At this rate, there won't be anything left for us to eat come midnight." She wrinkles her nose at me. "We respectfully wait until everyone is asleep to fill our banshee bellies. And could you please keep your mother's B&B better stocked with your goodies? I'm not spending my calorie free days eating celery and carrots."

"You bet," I say. "And what's this death day business you were whispering about?"

Greer tugs at a long glossy lock of her see-through hair. "Lottie, I died on Valentine's Day." She coos to Winslow, "Isn't that romantic? I had always wished February fourteenth was my birthday, but to have it as my death date is so much better."

I shake my head. "How do you figure?"

She waves me off. "Everyone knows you'll be dead a heck of a lot longer than you'll ever be alive."

"I guess I can't argue with you there."

Winslow chuckles and wraps an arm around her. "We hope you'll join us for the celebration of her afterlife, Lottie."

Greer nods. "We're still working on a venue, but we'll keep you posted."

"Sounds great. Swing by the bakery and we'll hammer out the details of that cake for you."

I speed into the kitchen just in time to see Keelie showing off her bare belly to a startled Jodie McCloud.

"Jodie." I quickly tug down Keelie's shirt and give her adorable budding belly a pat. "So nice to see you! We met at the community center the other day." I wince. "How are you holding up?"

She averts her eyes. Jodie is beautiful with a light peppering of freckles sprinkled over her nose and pale blue eyes.

"Patricia's mother has all but taken over the bakery. I'm right back to being a lackey again."

"I bet her mother is so distressed she doesn't know what to do with herself. I bet throwing herself into the bakery is her way of dealing with her grief."

"Oh, she's not grieving." A husky chuckle comes from her. "Deana and Patricia have been at each other's throats for as long as I've known them. I realize it's hard to believe, but some women don't seem to have a maternal gene and Deana happens to be one of them."

Keelie clutches her belly. "I hope I have a maternal gene."

"You will, Keelie." I pat her arm. "She's talking about women like Suze."

Keelie lifts a finger. "Makes total sense now." She takes up the platters from the Sweet Sin Bakery. "I'd best get these out there before the book club begins. Those ladies love to nosh while they read all the naughty bits out loud."

She whizzes past us, and I realize my window with Jodie is about to close.

"Have you ever been to one of these book clubs?" I ask. "You should check it out. It's a riot a minute with my mother and her friends."

A warm laugh bounces from her. "I think I'll pop my head in for a minute or two. I always like to make sure the cookies are a hit before I leave."

"Sounds good." A knot builds in my stomach and I can feel the questions begging to bubble out of me. "Can I ask you something? The other night you seemed pretty offended when Patricia introduced you as her assistant. Was Patricia pretty hard to get along with?" I figured that was a safer question than coming right out and asking if she killed her.

Jodie lets out a heavy sigh. "Hard to get along with just scratches the surface to describe her. She was impossible. Did you know that two years ago I was fully ready and willing to get my own bakery going? Patricia and I met in pastry school. She wanted to go into business with me and it all penciled out in the beginning, but what I didn't realize was that Patricia was going to take over her mother's bakery, hijack the name I had for my own, and make me work under her as kitchen help."

"I'm so sorry. So Sweet Sin was the name you picked out?"

"Yup." She gives a wistful shake of the head. "Patricia had me pay to help with the upgrades that her mother's rundown bakery needed, and that's where my business loan went. But once we got things going, it was clear who was going to be the top baker around there. After that it was tension city. My brother is a lawyer in Wisconsin and he was going to help me get out of the legal end of our arrangement, but now that she's dead, I guess I'll have to deal with her mother. And you want to hear something? Her mother is far worse than Patricia ever was. She's having the signage switched out today to read Patricia's Pastries once again. She always hated the name Sweet Sin. And she's giving me my walking papers. She says I have two weeks to find another job. You wouldn't happen to have any openings at your place, would you?"

I wince. "I don't actually." A thought comes to me. "But—I do have a lodge right there in Hollyhock that might be in need of a baker. I can check." Everett, Noah, and I happen to own the Maple Meadows Lodge that we purchased last December. Everett and I purchased it when Noah was incapacitated in a coma because we knew it was a piece of property he had his eye on. And, of course, once Noah came to, he insisted on buying Everett out, but it was too late at that point. Everett was so enamored with the lodge, himself, he wouldn't sell, but we did have Noah's name put on the title.

"Hollyhock?" Her eyes brighten. "Oh, Lottie. That means I wouldn't have to move. It was hard enough finding a rental that would allow cats the first time."

"Well, I'm a cat lover, too. Say no more." We start to make our way out of the kitchen. "So, Jodie, who do you think would be angry enough to kill both Whitney and Patricia?"

She shakes her head. "I don't know, but Patricia had enemies. I was just the tip of the iceberg when it came to people she ticked off."

"Was there anyone at the community center that night that she might have been going at it with?"

She tips her head to the side thoughtfully. "There's Larissa."

"Larissa Miller?" I inch back a notch with surprise. "The event coordinator for Vermont's Best Baker?"

"Yup. She came around the bakery a few times and they would step outside to talk. Each time Patricia came back in she looked flustered. I have no idea what that was about, but there was definitely something afoot. But then, Patricia had oodles of people outside of the baking biz who weren't happy with her either. Although, I doubt Larissa would be angry enough to gun down two contestants. And by the way, the Sweet Sin is still eligible to participate in the contest and I've decided to go ahead and do it. I figured if I win the title, it couldn't hurt for when I really do open up my own bakery."

"Sounds like some solid forward thinking. Good luck to you and may the best baker win."

We make our way into the sitting room in my mother's B&B. It's toasty and brimming with women—of every age—all looking rather eager to discuss their next dicey literary selection. I'm a bit surprised to see that both my sisters, Meg and Lainey, and my half-sisters, Kelleth and Aspen, are here.

Last summer, when I found out that Mayor Nash was my father, I gained three half-siblings, two sisters and a brother named Finn.

But aside from my sisters, I recognize Britney, Cormack, and Cressida—all of which reside at the B&B—Naomi and Lily, Eliza and Suze, Everett, Carlotta, and even Princess and Taffy are here as well.

Figures. Princess is so hypnotized by the male species she probably followed Everett right into the room. She brings new meaning to the words *sex kitten*. I crane my neck in her direction.

Hey? I do believe that's Thirteen by her side. She might just get a Valentine to call her own yet.

And, of course, there's Taffy. The pink and white spotted spectral snake is happily situated over Carlotta's shoulders. Last night, they spent an hour yacking about the mob and all things illegal that Leeds, a town just south of us, has to offer. Suffice it to say, Taffy has made Carlotta promise to take him to this golden land she spoke of. Come to think of it, Taffy might be the best friend Carlotta has ever had. It would figure that the one creature Carlotta gets along best with is a python.

I excuse myself from Jodie as I make my way over to Keelie.

"What's everyone doing here?" I whisper.

Keelie fans me with a hardback edition of today's selection, and I catch a quick glance at the sultry looking cover. There's a picture of a man with his billowy white shirt torn open and across his chest it reads *His Body on Fire*. I have a feeling the women who were reading this got a little hot and bothered themselves.

"The book clubs merged," Keelie whispers. "Our mothers were open to it as long as Naomi agreed to throw in a historical novel once in a while."

"Makes sense." Naomi was in charge of what she recently dubbed the Naughty Hottie Book Club. But seeing that both book clubs appreciated some steam, I totally get it.

Naomi scuttles this way and takes a seat next to her twin before swatting my hand. "The Evergreen Manor is hosting a couples' night on V-Day. It's called Love at the Evergreen. We need cake and cookies. Make it happen, would you?"

I blink back. "Why, I guess I will. Thank you for thinking of me, Naomi. So who's invited to this shindig? It sounds snazzy."

"It will be." Naomi nods assuredly, and this tidbit doesn't surprise me. Naomi has a taste for the finer things in life. "It's a last-minute thing I thought of. Half the proceeds will go to the sheriff's department in honor of one of the greatest loves of my life. My daddy."

"Aw! That's sweet," I say. Keelie and Naomi's father is the sheriff of Ashford County himself. "Count Noah and me in. Oh, and Everett, too." I'd feel terrible not inviting him.

"Everett is already going with Lily." Her lips expand dangerously wide, and my stomach sinks at the prospect of losing Everett to Lily for good.

"Okay, just Noah and me then."

Mom jumps to the front of the crowd and the room erupts with light applause.

"Thank you, thank you." She gives a mock bow. "We are very lucky to have a wonderful man by the name of Wiley Fox to join us here today. Please help me in welcoming him."

Another light round of applause ensues and I groan at the thought of her referencing him as wonderful. The man faked his own death, for Pete's sake. And for no apparent good reason.

I traipse my way to the front and take a seat next to Everett.

"And!" My mother lifts a finger in the air. "Wiley will be joining me today to help read a few passages from *His Body on Fire*."

"Nope." I don't even hesitate with the response, and Mom's lips contort in all sorts of crazy positions.

"But Lottie"—she whines—"that's part of the charm of having a man in the room. It will really help put a voice to Edwardo."

"Everett will put a voice to Edwardo. Both their names begin with E. It sounds like a closer match to me." I give the good judge a shove until he's standing in front of a crowd of howling women with his lids hanging low as if he were giving each and every one of them the bedroom eyes. Come to think of it, he's only looking at me.

Mom purrs his way as she pulls him close by the tie and the room starts howling once again.

Oh dear Lord. Am I really prepared to hear my mother reading dirty bits of who knows what with Everett? That will be something I will not only be unable to *unsee*, but I won't be able to *unhear* either.

"I'll take it from here," I say, jumping up and snatching the book from my mother's hand.

"Page one hundred and fifty-two, Lottie," Mom says it stern like a reprimand. "Try to put some feeling into it, would you?" She all but scowls at me before making herself scarce.

Everett and I start right in on the racy read, and neither of us hesitates to bring the red-hot passion to the table. To be perfectly honest, red-hot passion has always come naturally between Everett and me—and this red-hot moment is no exception.

Everett and I narrate the scene of Edwardo and Felicity's last tryst before Felicity will be married off to Edwardo's nemesis by her controlling father.

Everett's Edwardo does things to my Felicity that heats my body up ten thousand degrees—although, in truth, Everett's done all of those things and more with me behind locked doors. But it's nice to know we can give Edwardo and Felicity a run for their passionate money.

Soon enough, the entire room breaks out in applause— save for one handsome detective that looks as if he's ready to draw his weapon and kill.

The bodies in the room begin to mingle, and I take Everett by the hand as we make a beeline for Noah.

"It's not what it looks like," I pant. "Tell him, Everett."

"No," Everett says it flat. "It was exactly what it looks like. We were reading a book. If you can't handle that, Noah, then you've got problems I don't want to know about."

Noah's dimples depress, no smile. "I was actually hoping to speak with the two of you. I'm heading out to Fallbrook. I wanted to see if I could find Whitney's boyfriend, Chase Davis." He shoots a mean look to Everett. "I understand you were friends with the guy."

"That I was." Everett checks his phone. "I'm free."

"Good." Noah takes a deep breath. "It looks like I get to take Edwardo and Felicity to lunch. Lucky, lucky me."

I bite down on a smile. "You are lucky, Noah." I dot his lips with a kiss.

"He is," Everett agrees with me. "He's just too stubborn to see it."

And just like that, the three of us, along with a sexed-up kitten and an ornery snake, pile into Noah's truck as we head out to Fallbrook in hopes to catch a killer.

Chase Davis—what have you done?

That's exactly what we're about to find out.

6

Chase Davis owns a restaurant in Fallbrook called Mojitos that sits right outside the swanky downtown district of this ritzy town that both Noah and Everett once called home.

Everett wouldn't leave the B&B until he saw that Eliza was safe in her car and well on her way back to this neck of the woods herself. Noah couldn't do much about Suze, seeing that she lives at the B&B, but he figured she could hold her own. Heaven help us all if felony homicide charges are filed against her tonight. Come to think of it, Noah might actually look the other way with that one.

That leads me to Miranda Lemon. The spicy little tartlet made another clear pass at Wiley before we left, and, oddly enough, Carlotta made the man a juicy counteroffer. I wasn't going to stick around and try to referee my dueling mamas' private lives. That's why the good Lord gave me sisters.

Here's hoping Lainey and Meg can make heads or tails of this new mess my mother wants to dive into headfirst.

"After you," Everett insists as he holds the enormous wooden door to Mojitos open for both Noah and me.

Princess purrs dreamily at him as we walk through the door. "I like him, Lottie. He's awfully nice. I say we invite *Edwardo* over tonight for a little catnip and a game of chasing tails."

I swallow down a laugh. "Princess really likes you, Everett. I think you gained a fan with that spicy reading."

"I wasn't one of them," Noah is quick to get his point across.

Taffy sticks his forked little tongue out. "Me neither," he says while slithering his way across Noah's shoulders.

Inside, Mojitos looks like a little slice of tropical paradise with its imitation palm trees, a pale blue sky painted over the ceiling, and large screen televisions that play a scene from a white sandy beach on a loop.

"Now here's a nice switch compared to the polar blast we're experiencing outside," I say.

No kidding. It snowed five inches on the way over. It feels as if winter is here to stay, and she's not going to be dethroned any time soon.

Noah takes up my hand and kisses the back of it. "Maybe this is a good time to plan a tropical honeymoon?"

"Easy"—Everett displays a bored sense of agitation—"I think Lemon and I should decide where we go. I was thinking an extended European cruise, on a private yacht, of course."

"You're both funny," I say. But before I can properly reprimand Noah for so brazenly throwing a honeymoon in Everett's face, a waitress in a grass skirt and coconut bra leads us to a booth in the back.

I wait until she leaves to make my observations known. "It's nice to see that Chase insists on keeping it classy. I take it you summered with Chase as well?" He certainly summered with Cressida. And Lord knows Whitney was quick to throw their summer trysts in my face at my own wedding reception last month. The woman knew no shame.

Hey? Maybe that's what got her killed?

Noah gives my hand a squeeze. "I'm serious, Lottie. We should plan a vacation together. It might be good for us to get out of Honey Hollow. We should head for the lodge."

Princess purrs like a motorboat as she rolls her way to Noah. "You can take me anywhere you like, big boy. You just keep giving me those dimples and see how far it'll get you. I'll give you a hint—*everywhere*."

Noah lifts a brow her way.

"That's Princess," I say. "I've got two ghosts along for the homicidal ride. A fluffy white cat on a hot tin roof named Princess and a python bad boy named Taffy."

Taffy hisses directly into Noah's ear and he flinches.

"He's on me, isn't he? That's why I feel like I've got the weight of the world on my shoulders." Noah ducks and jives as if trying to rid himself of the slithering menace. But Taffy isn't a menace at all.

"He is," I say while picking up Everett's hand, too, so he can hear the dead as well, and suddenly it looks as if we're about to conduct a séance. "Sorry about that, Noah, but he's really taken a liking to you."

"Great." Noah nods to Taffy's tail as if it were his face.

"His head is actually to your right. I suppose it would help if the two of you could see the dead. Would you like that?"

"No," they both strum it out in unison.

"Ooh." Princess stretches out as if she felt that response right down to her ghostly bones. "Strong men who know what they like. This could be promising, Lottie. Take them both home."

"It doesn't work like that," I tell her. Although a devilish part of me wishes it did.

Princess tucks her nose in the air. "However it works, make sure we pick up Thirteen on the way home. That was one rough, tough, out of control handsome alley cat I'd like to make my own."

Everett tips his head. "Sounds like Princess could use a mojito to cool herself off." He cinches his cheek as he looks my way. "Pick your poison. I'm buying, Lemon. We've got a designated driver and my schedule is clear for the rest of the day."

"Sounds like a plan. Now that Carlotta is taking up residence in my back bedroom, a mojito sounds exactly like what I need to take the edge off, myself."

The waitress comes by and we each order a different version of the special of the day. Everett orders a house mojito and I order a peach one.

"So, Detective Fox"—I playfully butt my shoulder to Noah's—"how's the case going?"

Noah gives a long blink. "A double homicide unfortunately means double the work. It's hard to tell if the killer was after Whitney, Patricia, or both."

Everett strums his fingers over the table. "Don't forget Lemon."

Noah nods. "It's true, Lottie. They could have come after you. But seeing that they didn't give you the same fate as they gave their other victims, I don't know what to make of it. They either had put their weapon away and grabbed the nearest branch to knock you out with, or they didn't want to kill you."

"They may not have wanted to kill me that night, but someone sure wants me dead." I pull out my phone and show them a picture of that cookie that was delivered to my shop yesterday.

Both Noah and Everett fall into a mini rage over the fact it took me twenty-four hours to share this malfeasance with them.

"All right, all right," I say just as the waitress drops off our mojitos and an extra-large soda for Noah.

Taffy promptly sticks his entire head in Noah's dark carbonated treat, and soon half the volume disappears before our very eyes.

"Lottie?" Noah eyes the glass suspiciously. "Do I want to know?"

"Not really."

"Good." He offers me a stern look. "Because we can return the focus on you. That gun we gave you?"

"Ethel," I offer.

"Yes, Ethel," Everett says it curtly. "She's your new best friend. She's going with you everywhere."

Noah nods. "I'm sorry, Lottie. I know you like to keep the bakery a gun-free zone, but I think you should take Ethel there, too. Leave her in the deposit safe while you're working, but anytime you leave—I need to know you're protected. I'll make sure to station a deputy to Main Street, specifically to your bakery."

Everett grunts, "I'm hiring private security. Lemon, you're getting a security guard."

"*Ohh*, Lottie!" Princess pants as if the thought were too much. "Tell 'em to make it a big strong man with lots and lots of muscles," she moans that last word out with glee. "A nice long tail wouldn't hurt either."

Taffy scoffs. "Can someone put a rat in her mouth already? She never stops. It's bordering on offensive." He slithers over to Everett's drink and I bat him away.

"I don't need a security guard," I say. "A deputy on Main Street is probably fine."

"See that?" Everett pins Noah with a look. "She knows your deputies won't be around much. That's why she's agreeing to it."

Noah's dimples dig in. "You're right. I'll go in halves for the private guard."

I'm about to kick my protests into high gear when a tall man with a wide smile, shiny forehead, and an all-around jovial appeal pops over.

"How's everything going here?" His mouth widens as he looks to Everett. "Well, if it isn't Everett Hide-Your-Girlfriends Baxter!" He howls out a laugh while pulling Everett out of his seat and offering him one of those slapping man hugs.

They share a few laughs as they reminisce before the conversation grows dark.

Everett looks to Noah and me. "Chase, this is my wife Lottie and our neighbor Noah something or other."

Chase offers us each a polite shake before motioning for Everett to take a seat.

Everett scoots in and Chase fills in our booth.

"I'm sorry about Whitney." Everett shakes his head. "How are you doing, man?"

"Not good." His expression sobers up quickly. Odd, considering he was as happy as could be less than a few seconds ago. "You know we were set to marry last June."

"What?" Everett inches back. "I had no idea things were about to take a turn for the matrimonial with the two of you."

"I wanted it to." His eyes water as if on cue. "Two o'clock came on our special day and Whitney was a no-show. Just me and about a hundred close friends and family. It turns out, she went out for coffee that morning and ended up boarding a private jet to Palm Beach. I guess I wasn't the one for her after all."

"Oh, wow." My hand clutches over my chest. "I can't imagine how hard that must have been for you."

"It wasn't a picnic getting the news. She finally texted my brother at three. I had to tell the guests it was off myself. Of course, I invited everyone to stay and enjoy the steak and lobster dinner. No use in letting all that food go to waste." He closes his eyes a moment. "And since I had the band ready to go, there was dancing as well. All wasn't lost, though. My little brother ended up meeting the love of his life that night and they're getting married same time next June." His expression sours. "That is, if Jenny bothers to show up."

Princess grunts, "Poor thing. He needs a good woman in his life. One that knows how to treat a man." An elongated purr strums from her.

Taffy groans, "Let me guess. That would be you? For heaven's sake, Lottie, find this feline a warm body before we all go stark raving mad."

Princess swats Taffy over the face with her tail. "Warm isn't a requirement for me these days."

I take a quick breath as I try to revert my attention back to Chase.

"I'm so sorry to hear that," I tell him. "Did you and Whitney ever get the chance to patch things up?"

He stares out at the wall across the way. "No. Whitney came back and threw herself at whoever she pleased—whoever wasn't me."

"What about her bakery?" I ask. "Did she throw herself into her work? The Upper Crust seems to be quite a hit out this way."

His brows jump as if it were news to him. "Whitney never threw herself into her work. Whitney simply doesn't work. She wouldn't know pie dough from cake batter. Whitney had never baked anything in her life." He turns to Everett. "Did you ever see her in the kitchen?"

"Come to think of it"—Everett shakes his head—"no, I didn't."

Taffy slithers his way over to Chase and glides right up the front of his shirt, inciting Chase to give himself a scratch.

"I smell hatred," Taffy hisses it out. "Ask if he killed the girls. If so, I'll constrict his ribcage right this minute and save everyone a lot of time and effort."

I shake my head just enough for the slippery serpent to see it.

"Chase?" I start off sweetly. "When was the last time you saw Whitney?"

He shifts his gaze to the front door as if he were eyeing the exit. "Last week. Communication between the two of us was sparse. I thought maybe if I hired her to cater the Valentine's event we're having here, maybe we could get that spark back."

Everett sighs. "And how did that go?"

"Not well." Chase hardens his lips. "Whitney started flirting with my night manager right in front of me." He scoffs. "Let's just say that's when the blinders finally came off and I realized that she would never change. Ruthie was right. Whitney had zero regard for other people's feelings. It was all about her, all the time." He blows out a heavy breath. "But I'm not telling you anything you don't know, Everett."

Everett leans in. "I'm sorry, who's Ruthie?"

"Ruthie Beasley. Whitney's personal assistant," Chase offers. "She also happens to be in charge of the bakery.

Whitney figured with Ruthie at the helm she could hide the fact she wasn't responsible for all those pastries."

A waitress comes by and whispers something in his ear.

"I'd better get going." He shakes Everett's hand and does the same with Noah and me. "Enjoy the food. It's on me today."

"Thank you," we say in unison, and I give Everett a light kick under the table.

Everett lifts a finger his way. "Chase? What do you think happened that night?"

Chase looks to the ceiling a moment. "Easy. I heard there were two girls that were gunned down and a third injured. All three of them were bakers set to compete in some big bake-off coming up. I think someone wanted to bump off the competition. If I were the Ashford Sheriff's Department, I'd talk to the one that survived with nothing but a simple knock to her head. She's probably the one that did it. Nice attempt at trying to make herself look like a victim. And if she happens to own a gun—well, that would be the clincher. It's an open and shut case, if you ask me." He nods to us all before taking off, and both Taffy and Princess chortle in his wake.

"Did you hear that? He's pointing the finger at me," I say, incensed.

Noah takes a deep breath. "I won't lie, Lottie. Ivy still has your picture up on the suspect board."

I roll my eyes at that one.

Just the thought of Ivy Fairbanks makes my stomach roll. I have it on good authority she has the hots for Noah. Honestly? Who could blame her?

"Well, I didn't do it."

Everett swirls his drink in his hand. "Ruthie sounds like she had a reason to be angry."

Noah nods. "So does your buddy. Do you think he's capable of something like this?"

Everett winces. "His heart was sold on her for as long as I knew it. He's always been just this side of obsessed with Whitney."

"Obsessed?" My eyes widen with the revelation.

"Nothing twisted, I don't think." Everett looks momentarily distressed. "I can't see him gunning her down. It's been over nine months since that wedding fiasco. And then there was Patricia. Killing two women in cold blood doesn't sound like the Chase Davis I once knew."

"People change," Noah says just as our food arrives.

"So I guess Ruthie is next on the list." I look to Noah for affirmation, and he's slow to shake his head.

"I'm sorry, Lot." Noah's dimples dig in, no smile. "This one cut too close to home. If there's a baker out there bumping off the competition, sending you death threats, the last thing I'm going to do is feed you to the lions. I'm officially taking you off the case."

Everett nods. "And I'm officially agreeing with him."

I lift my mojito and take a quick sip of its tropical goodness.

Fine. They can have it their way. But it just so happens that my mother is hosting her matchmaker mixer tomorrow night, and I think I'll need one more bakery to help with the catering. I'm thinking the Upper Crust Bake Shop will do.

It's not my fault if I just so happen to bump into Ruthie Beasley.

And for the record, I won't be investigating. I'll simply be shooting the breeze with one of my esteemed colleagues.

Who knows? We might even get around to exchanging recipes—or swapping theories about a certain double homicide that's momentarily thrown both of our lives off the rails.

I'll be sure to shake everything out of Ruthie that she's willing to give me.

Even if it's murder.

7

True to Noah and Everett's word, the very next day I have an ultra-muscular, ultra-creepy security guard stationed right outside my bakery.

The guard in question is a tall, beefy, bald man with eyes that prowl the vicinity as sure as lasers. I've tried to ask his name and tried to get him to smile. I've tried to give him a cookie, but it's as if I'm invisible to him. Everett told me they instructed him not to commingle with anyone whatsoever unless he's suspicious of them. And so far, this six-foot-five wall of muscles has been suspicious of no one.

But the day is done, the bakery is closed, and it's time to take all of the sweet treats I've baked for my mother's matchmaker mixer and deliver them to her B&B. I've even baked a three-tiered cake covered in fondant that I've scored to give it a quilted appeal. The bottom tier is red, the middle tier is fuchsia, and the top tier is a soft baby pink, topped off with a bouquet of my conversation heart cookies.

Everett showed up just as Lily and I were about to pull away and followed us to the B&B to help offload all the goodies.

The conservatory in my mother's B&B is illuminated with just enough light to set the right mood for all things romantic. The entire cavernous space is festooned with pink and red hearts everywhere you look. Her tiny bistro tables are strewn about, and each one is dotted with a votive candle with a flame dancing and flickering inside.

Smooth and easy love songs stream through the speakers overhead, and the throngs of bodies already filling the room have wasted no time in swaying to the music. Even the ghosts are having a good time. Greer and Winslow are currently slow dancing near the crystal chandelier my mother has hanging up above. Thirteen and Princess have been frolicking away in a ghostly game of cat and mouse. And little Lea has been stalking the room while whipping Taffy around by the tail. I'll admit that Lea's treatment of Taffy looks disconcerting, but every now and again he lets out a righteous howl of delight that assures me he's having the time of his nonexistent life.

And since my sisters helped with the decorations, both of them have decided to stick around with their plus ones. Lainey and Forest are slow dancing to the music. Meg and her boyfriend, Hook Redwood, look as if they're conducting some sort of wrestling takedown of one another. Hook runs his family's real estate empire along with the finance firm he's started with Noah's brother, Alex.

Speaking of Noah's playboy of a sibling, he's already swift on his feet with Naomi Turner while Lily looks red as a fire engine in the corner.

Keelie told me that as soon as their mother mentioned the event, Naomi knew Lily would be here setting up the sweet treats, so Naomi being her devilish self, invited Alex out for a romantic night on the town.

Poor Lily. It wouldn't surprise me at all if Honey Hollow were hit with another double homicide. If I were Naomi and Alex, I'd watch my back.

"Thank you for helping, Everett," I say as we set the very last platter into place. Everett looks stunning tonight in his sharp suit and bright red tie. Most of the women here have slowly migrated his way to get a better look at the sexy judge in our midst. Everett has a way of stealing the spotlight from just about every male wherever he goes.

"I'm always ready and willing to help you."

I crimp my lips up at him. "Me? I thought you came by to help Lily." I couldn't help letting the dig fly. I'm still not over the fact he'll be going to the Love at the Evergreen event with Lily as his date.

Everett's lips twitch as he does his best to contain a smile. Everett has never been one to curve his lips in the right direction freely. Every smile he gives is few and far between and hard-won to boot.

"I'm here for you, Lemon. It's always you."

Now it's me twitching my lips, only I don't know whether to laugh or cry.

"Everett, I know Lily will be your date at the Evergreen on Valentine's Day. And I just want you to know that's okay." My voice cracks when I say that last word as if it were anything but okay.

Everett tips his head to the side. His lips pull back as he examines me with those searing blue flames he calls eyes.

"Can I have this dance, Lemon?"

"Dance?" My eyes widen as I glance next to us where couples sway slowly as they talk amongst themselves and laugh. "Yeah, sure." My stomach cinches as Everett takes me in his arms, navigating us deep into the crowd as the room seems to grow darker by the minute.

Everett pulls me close to him by the small of my back, and I can feel his powerful heartbeat ricocheting over my body like thunder.

"This is nice," I say as I press my lips tight in fear I tell him exactly how nice I'm finding it.

"This is nice," he whispers it close to my ear, and the entire left side of my body ignites like fire. "See that?" He nods over to Alex and Naomi, and I can't help but frown. "That's why Lily asked me to the Evergreen on Valentine's Day. She wants Alex to see her in a red dress designed specifically to make him sweat."

I take in a breath as my cheeks burn bright. "Of course." I exhale with a small laugh, but I quickly sober up once again. "Everett. If you wanted to—you know, see someone..." I shrug because I can't bring myself to finish the sentence.

His brows dip, meeting in the middle, looking like a bird in flight.

"I have a confession." He pulls back with his lids hanging low. "I am very much seeing someone."

"Who is she?" The words speed out of me so quick it sounds like a hiss.

Everett doesn't say a word. He simply dots my nose with a kiss, and I can feel myself blushing all over again.

Someone gives Everett's shoulder a tap from behind, and he steps back to expose Noah Corbin Fox in his tweed jacket and dark jeans, a dimpled grin breaking out on his handsome face just for me.

Noah tips his head to the side. "Mind if I cut in?"

My lips part as I look to Everett.

He gives a slight nod. "Take your time, Lemon. If you took a million years, I wouldn't go anywhere."

Before he can leave, Mom bops up wearing a tight red dress and a matching headband pressed into her hair with twin heart-shaped antennae wobbling back and forth. She holds a tray of various cocktails before her, each a variant shade of pink.

She giggles our way. "Noah, did you know your father is a premier mixologist? He's so good, I've given him a position right here at the B&B."

"What?" I hiss. "You hired Wiley to work for you as a bartender?"

"No way." Noah shakes his head.

Everett nods. "I'll take care of this."

"Oh no, you don't," my mother is quick to snap. "The man is in need of honest employment and I happen to have a position that needed to be filled."

"*Mother.*" I shake my head at her. "You run a B&B. People sip on cocoa and cider by the fire. Nobody has ever requested hard liquor here and you know it."

She waves me off. "That's because it wasn't readily available. Now, how would you like a fresh and frosty concoction? We've got a cloud nine, strawberry sweetheart, love potion, sweet seduction, pink crush, Romeo and Juliet— and Wiley's drink of the night, Mirandy Lemony Lemonade."

A hard groan comes from me. "Please tell me you haven't been letting him read your racy fiction." My mother's pen name happens to be Mirandy Lemonade. She's yet to publish her foray into literature, but she freely distributes copies to unfortunate friends and family.

"Oh, Lottie, must you be so crass? Of course, I haven't. But I do leave copies of my work in the sitting room, available for the viewing pleasure of anyone who happens to come across them. And should he have come across a copy, then so be it." She gives a sly wink my way as she pushes her tray farther our way, and out of the blue pop two thin, pale arms as they each snatch a drink right off it.

The thin, pale arms happen to belong to Cressida Bentley and Cormack Featherby. They both look dazzling in matching pink and silver sequin dresses. I'm about to make a quip about them looking like disco ball inspired bookends when I spot a curious sight at the door.

Serena Digby, wicked witch extraordinaire, is speaking to a shorter redheaded girl that I recognize from the community center the other night. It's Ruthie Beasley holding a platter of treats from the Upper Crust Bake Shop.

My mouth opens as I look to Everett and Noah. If I tell them about my plan to interrogate Ruthie, they'll crush it like a tin can.

Cormack latches onto Noah and Cressida does the same to Everett and the two gentlemen do their best to rebuff the glittery girls.

"Oh, what's one dance?" I say as both Noah and Everett widen their eyes my way.

Cressida sucks in a quick breath as she smacks her partner in curses crime. "The spell is working!"

Cormack huffs my way as she wraps her arms around Noah like a python. "Of course, it's working. Laronda, go fetch yourself something to eat." She turns back to Noah, as her lips curl with wicked intent. "We're too busy to think about food. Our appetites are far more carnal than that."

Noah shoots a suspicious look my way, and I quickly lose myself in the crowd. I figure I have less than ten minutes before Everett and Noah break free from the stronghold their exes have over them.

"Ruthie!" I say and the friendly looking redhead seems momentarily confused. "We met at the community center. I can help you set those down." I steal a second to glare at the witch by my side. "Serena." I frown over at her. "Looking for a chance at love?"

She shakes her head as if the concept were silly. "I can have any man I want, Lottie." She nods behind me and I turn to find Alex and Naomi.

"Oh, dear Lord, anything but that."

"Just watch how quickly I make him mine." She saunters off in a barely-there black dress that clings to her in all the right places, but I don't stick around for the fireworks.

Serena Digby has never met the likes of Naomi Turner. If she thinks this will be easy, that witch has another thing coming.

Instead, I put the platter down and quickly usher Ruthie into the hall.

"Thank you so much for coming all the way out here. My mother and I wanted to show some support for the Upper Crust. How are you doing? I know this must be hard for you."

"Hard?" Her green eyes round out like silver dollars. "I've never been so relieved in all my life. Whitney was a taskmaster like no other. I've actually quit taking my anxiety meds, and I've had a better night's sleep this last week than I've had in years. It didn't take a rocket scientist to figure out that the root of my problems was caused by Whit."

"Wow, I didn't realize she was so hard to work for."

"Hard would have been welcomed. She was mean through and through. She had zero problem putting me down in front of both her friends and mine. I think it made her feel more important."

A pink jag of supernatural lightning ignites, and Taffy lands himself over her shoulders.

"Did she do it?" Taffy hisses while sticking his flat, forked tongue right into her ear.

Princess and Thirteen trot this way.

"Oh, Lottie." Princess scampers up the side of my body and lands on my own shoulder—and I'd swear on all that is holy I feel her heft every bit as if she were real. "Tell me you didn't solve the case so soon. Thirteen has yet to show me what he can do with a mixing bowl."

I look down at the ebony-colored cat with a morbid curiosity as to what that might be.

Taffy gives them both a vicious hiss. "Never mind the tawdry twosome. Get on with the questioning. I want Patricia's killer to myself so I can offer them a proper embrace."

I make a face at his homicidal offer.

"Ruthie, who do you think was capable of doing this to Whitney?"

She shakes her head. "It was more than just Whitney. It could have been someone coming after the other girl. And to think, Whitney asked me to walk with them. Had I gone, I might have been the third victim."

Easily it could have been me as well.

"I agree it could have been someone angry with Patricia—and maybe Whitney simply got in the way, or maybe someone dealing with the bakers setting to compete. You haven't received any threats, have you?"

For the time being, I plan on keeping my dark cookie secrets to myself.

"Me?" She pokes a finger to her chest. "Nope. Like I said, I've never felt so stress-free in all my life. Just between you and me, I'm training other staff to take care of the bakery. I don't want anything to do with Whitney or anything that's left of her."

"Can I ask what's next for you?"

She glances to the conservatory and sighs. "I'm looking to work for myself. At least that way I can assure myself I won't have another rotten boss to contend with. I have a little money tucked away. I might just take a nice long cruise while I consider my options."

"A cruise? That sounds lovely." All sorts of bells and whistles are going off with that revelation. It sounds like Ruthie here is gearing up to get out of town, maybe for good.

"It will be lovely." Ruthie clenches her fists, and her lips knot up as she nods in agreement.

Princess sniffs as she leans close to my ear. "My, for someone professing to be worry-free, she sure seems anxious."

Taffy moans, "As much as I hate to agree with the flea trap, I think she may be onto something."

Princess dives over the sarcastic serpent, and soon they're wrestling it out, right over Ruthie's body.

Ruthie plucks at her sweater. "If you'll excuse me, I'm feeling a little warm. It was nice talking to you."

"You as well. Hey, Ruthie? Was there anyone at all you can think of that Whitney was at odds with?"

She tips her head to the side thoughtfully. "You know, that woman who was putting together the competition—Larissa something? She was coming around the shop quite a bit. And she always insisted on talking to Whitney directly."

My mouth falls open. It's the very same thing that Jodie told me.

"What do you think she wanted?"

Ruthie shrugs. "Something to do with the competition obviously. Has she spoken to you yet?"

"No, she hasn't." A thought comes to me. "Was Whitney ever visibly upset after their conversation?"

Ruthie purses her lower lip. "You know, come to think of it, she was in a sour mood. But that was Whitney most of the time. So I guess I can't really tell."

"Thanks for the heads-up about Larissa. I'll keep an eye out for her." If I don't track her down first. "Hey, will the Upper Crust still be competing?"

"You bet. I'll be doing the baking myself. A friendly warning, I plan on leaving my time as a baker on a high note." She gives a little giggle. "May the best baker win."

"May the best baker win, indeed."

I watch as she takes off and try my best to make sense of the pieces she just offered up, but right now it's about as clear as mud.

"Lottie?" Thirteen calls from the reception counter, and both Princess and Taffy stop their frolicking long enough to follow me over. "It seems there's a package for you."

My heart stops as I spot the familiar looking little black bag. I head over and dip my hand into the tissue paper and pull out a heart-shaped cookie iced in black. There, in hot pink print, it reads *death becomes you*.

Before I can process it, both Noah and Everett flank me on either side.

There's no hiding this one.

They've already seen it.

The killer wants to add another victim to their list—and that victim would be me.

8

There have been times I've been thrilled to be curled up by the fire with my cats and not another human in the world. Tonight is not one of those. Thankfully, both Everett and Noah decided that having a picnic in my living room was an excellent idea.

Once I discovered yet another scrumptious looking threat—or more to the point, once Noah and Everett discovered the confection-based malfeasance, they quickly ensconced me in bubble wrap and rolled me home.

Okay, fine, not really. But it was close enough. I hardly had time to say goodbye to my sisters. Both Noah and Everett threatened Wiley to stay away from the far too friendly owner of the B&B. And, of course, I took the time to appropriately threaten my mother to stay away from any men who may have recently come back from the dead.

All that being said, both Noah and Everett threatened one another plenty on the way to the car over what restaurant to stop off at and pick up takeout.

Noah and I ended up stopping at Mangias and picking up a couple of large pizzas, and Everett stopped off at the Wicked Wok and loaded up on enough Chinese food to satiate a frat house.

And the three of us meet up again on Country Cottage Road, right on my front porch to be exact. Noah actually lives right across the street. It was Noah who lived on Country Cottage Road first. We were dating at the time I was in serious need of a roof over my head, and he happened to have not one but two rental houses available right across the street from him. And as fate would have it, I took one and Everett took the other. Everett lives in a split-level next door to me, and the three of us are a trifecta of perfection. Okay, more of a devil's triangle, but that's beside the point.

I invited Noah to bring his golden retriever, Toby, over as well, but he says he'll bring him over after we eat or we'll have to contend with some serious begging. Toby has the biggest brown eyes you ever did see, and Noah is well aware of the fact that I've never been able to deny him a slice of Mangias pizza.

"Let me get the key out," I say, struggling to pluck it from my purse.

Everett grunts, "You should always have your key ready to go before you leave your car, Lemon. That way you can get into the house as quickly as possible."

"Hear that?" Noah's chest pumps a dry laugh. "He's the kind of guy that likes to tell you what to do. Don't sign up for a lifetime of that, Lottie." Noah pulls out his phone and turns the flashlight on. "You really should leave your porch light on when you know you're going to be out late."

I pause my rummaging pursuit long enough to shoot Noah a look.

"Okay, fine," he says. "I'm just as guilty. Here"—he shines the light in my purse—"I see it." He fishes in my bag a moment before coming up victorious.

"See that?" Everett quips. "Not only will he tell you what to do, but he'll take over and show you how to do it. Don't sign up for a lifetime of that, Lemon."

A tiny giggle bubbles up my throat, but just as Noah is about to put the key into the lock, a flash of light shines out from the living room window.

"What in the heck?" I hiss in fear.

Noah looks to Everett. "Get Lottie to the car." He puts the pizzas on the porch and pulls his weapon from its holster, motioning for us to get down.

"I'm not going anywhere," I whisper as the flashlight coming from the inside of my house shines over the neighborhood haphazardly. "GAH! My babies are in there!

Poor Pancake and Waffles must be frightened out of their furry minds!"

Noah shakes his head to Everett. "I'm going in alone."

Before I know it, I'm in Everett's arms and Noah bursts through the door—with the key, of course— weapon drawn.

"*Freeze!*" he riots it out so loud I can feel his voice reverberating right down to my bones. "Ashford County Sheriff's Department!" he howls, slapping the light switch as he jumps inside. The house blinks to life with a peachy glow, and the sound of a woman screaming ricochets into the night.

Both Everett and I lean toward the door out of a morbid curiosity, and our eyes will never be the same.

"Oh my goodness!" I belt it out like a threat as I shake myself free from Everett and step into the house.

Noah stands frozen in a defensive stance with his gun drawn and pointed at a quasi-shirtless man wearing a ski mask.

"Take it off," Noah barks.

The man tips his head this way. "The shirt or the mask?" It comes out garbled.

"The mask," Noah demands, and in less than five seconds, an all too familiar face is revealed.

"Mayor Nash?" I wail it out like a protest.

Carlotta slowly steps forward with her hands held high, her fuzzy pink robe opened in the front, and nothing but a flesh-colored wrinkly old gray sweatshirt on under—

Both Everett and Noah let out a horrific groan.

Suffice it to say, I was wrong about the wrinkly gray sweatshirt.

"What's the matter, boys?" Carlotta quickly covers up and cinches her belt. "It's been a while since you've seen a woman in the flesh, huh?" She practically snarls my way. "Don't blame me. I didn't raise her."

"Good grief," I say, stepping inside, only to find both Pancake and Waffles sleeping soundly on the sofa. "Thank goodness," I whisper just as I spot a trio of glowing orbs floating near the fireplace. It's Princess, Thirteen, and Taffy.

The charming snake rolls and slithers his way through the air. "We beat you home by a mile. You missed quite the show."

"Well, I don't want to hear about it," I say it low for their ears only.

Noah steps in deeper into the room. "What is going on?"

Everett's chest thumps. "Excuse him, but he really does need a road map."

Carlotta rolls her eyes. "Careful there, Detective. There's a tub of hot wax about five inches from you on that sofa table. I'd hate to see you get burned in all the wrong places."

"Carlotta," I say, staggering forward and observing my crockpot being used for both nefarious and carnal purposes. "I'm sorry, but you've gone too far. I forbid you to use my home as a perverted playground. It's not right. Not to mention, someone could get seriously hurt."

Carlotta grunts as she stalks off toward Mayor Nash.

"Come on, Harry. Now that the kid is home, all of our fun will be relegated to my bedroom."

Mayor Nash hustles along while his fingers fiddle to button up his shirt.

"I was playing the part of the intruder," he starts and the three of us each raise a hand as if silently begging him to stop. "And Carlotta was going to crack a pan over the top of my head and tie me to the kitchen chair."

"A pan?" I look to Carlotta with wild eyes. "Carlotta, you could have killed him."

She scoffs at the thought. "Well then, it looks like you showed up right on time." She curls a finger toward the fireplace. "Come on, Taffy. I know when we're not wanted." And sure enough, the supernatural serpent glides right on down the hall with her.

Princess stretches out, arching her back dramatically, and I'd swear on all things good and right that I just saw Thirteen drool like a *thirteen*-year-old boy.

Princess hops on his back. "Take me to see the best show in town, tiger. It might just inspire me."

And like a flash of onyx lightning, Thirteen has them to Carlotta's bedroom faster than Carlotta gets there herself.

Mayor Nash lifts a finger as he spots Everett hauling in two large pizza boxes and a bag full of Wicked Wok.

"Say, have you got a couple slices you can spare? Having a gun drawn on me really gets my appetite going, and Mangias would hit the spot right about now."

"Take an entire box," I say, handing one over, and he thanks me before taking off and sequestering himself in the back bedroom.

"That wasn't awkward at all," I say, kicking my boots off as Everett builds a fire.

Noah puts his weapon up high on the dining room hutch. It's exactly where he always puts his gun when he comes over. I keep Ethel in my underwear drawer. I figure if I need her in the middle of the night she'll be more accessible to me that way. But I have a feeling after tonight's cookie fiasco, Noah will be accessible to me that way and he'll be a lot closer than my underwear drawer.

The three of us gather around the fire and indulge in a smorgasbord of pizza and Chinese food while I try to talk about anything but the case or my newfound stalker.

Noah finishes up his last bite and washes it down with a bottle of water.

"Lottie"—he scoots in close to me—"for your own protection, I think I should move in for a while—just until I have a chance to apprehend the killer."

Everett's brows hike up a notch. "Lemon, I'd take a look at his track record as far as apprehending killers is concerned, and then I would seriously consider charging him rent."

Noah's lids hang low with a quiet rage. "And what do you propose? Let me guess. You think you should move in, instead."

"Nope." Everett ticks his head to the side. "I think she should move into my place lest she runs into Mayor Nash in the buff while he's on his way to the restroom."

A horrific groan comes from me. "And judging by tonight, it's a real possibility."

Noah inches back as he looks to Everett. "You mean she should move to my place."

"Nope." Everett gives a playful smile that's far too short-lived. "I have a feeling that your dear old pops won't have a place to stay for long. And unless you want him freezing solid in the snow, you'll have to take him in. You don't want to be responsible for his untimely death, do you?"

"It's tempting." Noah doesn't miss a beat. "And not that this scenario is happening, but what makes you think he won't be staying with Alex?"

Everett shrugs. "Alex wisely moved into a one-bedroom condo that overlooks Honey Lake. It's a bachelor pad if ever there was one. You've got two bedrooms to spare. You're older. Face it. You're the unwanted parent by default. And you're a good guy. You'll do it and stuff the pain." He gives a sly wink my way. "You won't have to suffer, Lemon. I've got a room for you, en suite, with a walk-in closet and a tub the size of your sofa."

I bite down on my lip as I consider the tempting offer. Truth is, I'm far too familiar with Everett's oversized tub. However, the last time I was in it, there were two of us splashing around.

A rush of heat spirals through me at the thought, and I shake it right out of my head.

"About that killer." I clear my throat. "Why do you think they're stalking me?"

Noah bows his head a moment before coming up for air. "I don't know, Lot. I've been beating myself up trying to get to the bottom of this. All I can think of is that they're afraid you might know who it is and they're using the threats as an intimidation tactic to keep you quiet."

"Oh, if I knew, I wouldn't be quiet about it. I'd turn them in."

Everett nods. "And I'm betting they know that. They might be testing you."

"Well, this is one test I'm not interested in passing. I want them behind bars, and I want it done yesterday. Catch them, Noah," I say. "And make it fast. I won't lie. It's terrifying to think they know where I work, where my mother lives." I suck in a quick breath. "I bet they know where I live, too."

Noah's dimples depress as he stares off, deep in thought. "I don't get it, though. Why toy with you? I mean, they've already killed two people."

"Noah!" I swat him. "Are you asking why they don't just bump me off?"

Pancake and Waffles slowly meander down to our circle, and I take Pancake and Everett takes Waffles. Trust me when I say, there is nothing hotter than a man snuggling with one of your sweet fluffy cats.

Noah nods. "That's kind of what I'm saying. I mean, why all the head games? If you know the sheriff's department isn't onto you, why not skip town?"

Everett takes a breath. "Because if Lemon happens to remember something that points to an individual and that individual is suddenly on a permanent vacation, the homicide detectives in charge might actually put two and two together."

"Ooh, that reminds me. I spoke to Ruthie Beasley tonight"—I wince over at Noah—"long story. Anyway, she mentioned that as soon as Vermont's Best Baker wraps up, she's taking off. I think she mentioned a cruise. She said she's training someone to take over her duties at the Upper Crust."

Noah pulls his phone out and makes a note. "Sounds like Ruthie is about to skip town. I'll have to look into this further." His brows dip into a hard V as he glowers my way. "Lottie, I meant it when I said that you shouldn't be alone."

I shrug over at him. "I've got Carlotta. On second thought, that might be worse than being alone. I think maybe you *should* move in until we catch the killer."

"Until *I* catch the killer," he pleads with his voice, with those evergreen eyes filled with angst.

Everett exhales hard. "And I'll keep an eye out on things." He rises to his feet.

"Don't go." Now it's me who's pleading. "There's still plenty of pizza and Wicked Wok to plow through."

"Believe me, I've had enough." He lands a sweet kiss to the top of Waffles' head before he hands him to Noah. "Sleep with one eye open, Fox. You never know. It could be me breaking in. I've been known to wake up in strange places." He shoots Noah with his finger. "I might just smother you in your sleep."

I toss a throw pillow at him. "Now there's a charming bedtime story."

Everett's chest rumbles with a laugh. "I believe they call that a happily ever after." He gives a quick wink before heading out the door.

Noah's lips curve with devilish intent. "Our first night together as roommates. Whatever will we do to pass the time?"

"Seeing that we just had dinner, I'd say dessert is in order." I pull him over and land a lingering kiss to his lips. Noah Fox never fails to make my insides flutter, my knees melt, and my mind turn to mush. It must be love.

He sweeps me off my feet and dashes me to the bedroom.

Noah loves me like nobody's business well into the night.

And yet, we both sleep with one eye open.

Someone out there is sending me a message—a not-so sweet semi-murderous Valentine.

And if either Noah or I don't stop them—I might not make it to Valentine's Day after all.

My phone buzzes on my nightstand, and I pull it close as I squint at the screen.

"Oh my goodness, Noah."

9

It was a text from Suze.

Okay, so she didn't actually say anything—Lord knows I'm not worth the words to her. She sent a picture. A rather saucy, in-your-face exposé on what my mother was doing at the time—and what she was doing was getting way too frisky with that *Wiley* Fox.

It's clear that Wiley isn't afraid of either Noah or Everett's threats. And it's crystal clear that my mother has no regard for my opinion where her love life is concerned.

That racy picture flits through my mind—my mother with her dress askew while Wiley indulged himself over her neck.

My goodness, is the man a vampire?

Regardless, it was clear he was sinking his fangs into her.

Everett stopped by the bakery this morning on his way to the courthouse, and I shared the perverse picture with him. I asked his advice, and, of course, Everett, being the genius he is, suggested that Noah and I come at this from a different angle. He suggested we offer to take them both out on a double date.

I know. I *know*.

It's complete insanity.

But my mother jumped at the chance to further her nonexistent relationship with Wiley. And Noah said Wiley didn't protest either—but he did have one request. Apparently, there's a steak house in Hollyhock that he still has a mean hankering for and that's what brings the five of us right here to a restaurant called Crusty Creations—yes, *five*.

As soon as Suze got wind of the fact we were headed to Crusty's she hightailed it over to Hollyhock herself.

And here we sit, at a romantic table as an unwholesome quintet.

Crusty Creations is a dimly lit, romantic culinary destination with a menu that consists mostly of fried chicken and steak. Surprisingly, there's a dance floor, and easy music bleeds through the speakers, encouraging many a couple to spring right out of their seats. The walls are covered with navy velvet, the floors are comprised of stained plywood, and there seems to be a unique balance of elegant and trashy.

There's a metaphor tucked in there somewhere that can be squarely set on the Fox family shoulders, but I'm not touching it.

Instead, I reach over and pick up Noah's hand. Him I'll touch all day long—or more to the point, all night long.

"So, Suze—" Mom's lips twist with delight. Interesting footnote: Miranda Lemon is equally as delighted to have Suze accompany us as she is Wiley. "Tell me—did you happen to meet anyone special at last night's matchmaker mixer?"

"Mother." I can't help but make a face. How does she not see anything wrong with this? I mean, sure, Suze's heart has morphed into a block of concrete, but she was married to Wiley once. It's awkward enough she's a third wheel on her ex-husband's double date. But my mother now wants her to disclose who she might be having amorous affections for? "Please excuse her, Suze. I'm afraid my mother might have left her good senses back at the B&B." In the basement, buried six feet under in an impenetrable steel box that she no longer has the key to.

Suze waves me off. Both Suze and my mother have donned scarlet dresses and, I'll admit, the fashion faux pas is a bit unnerving considering the fact I've donned a red dress myself. We look like a trio of red-hot harlots ready to paint the town with the overused hue.

"Lottie, I don't care who your mother has chosen to pursue." Suze gets right to the point. "And if she feels the need to suction herself to a leech who is only after two things, then so be it."

Ha!

Maybe bringing Suze along for the ridiculous ride was ingenious.

I nod over to her. "And what would those two things be?" Spell it out, Suze, because my mother needs it in writing.

Noah picks up my hand and offers up a gentle squeeze. I can't tell if he's cheering me on or asking me to cool it. With this unpredictable crowd, it's probably both.

Suze smirks over at both my mother and Wiley, who also happen to be holding hands as if they had the right to. "Miranda, let the record show that I'm being perfectly honest with you. That man wants your body and your money—and not necessarily in that order."

"*Aha!*" I slap the table as if Suze had just given the winning answer on a quiz show—and, face it, she has. "See that, Mom?" I shake my head at her. "You need to get out while you can. Noah and I will take you home right now. Suze has her own car, and Wiley—well, maybe he can find both employment *and* shelter right here at Crusty's."

"*Lottie,*" Mom hisses it out fast and filled with fury before reverting to her sweet sanity-may-care previously scheduled programming. "Wiley, please excuse my daughter.

I'm afraid you'll have to win her trust. But once you have it, you'll have a friend for life."

This older version of the man I love gives a wistful shake of the head. "She's my daughter-in-law. I already love her as if she were my own child." He shoots a dimpled grin my way. "Lottie, don't you worry about your mother. I've got only my best intentions with her."

And that's exactly what I'm afraid of. Something tells me, Wiley and I define the word *best* in entirely different ways.

Noah clears his throat. "Dad, I think Lottie would be most comfortable if you pursued anyone other than her mother."

Wiley pulls my mother's hand to his lips and dots it with a kiss. "No can do, son. There's no one else for me but this little lady right here. If I have my way, you and I will both be wed to Lemon women."

A horrible groan works its way up my throat just as Suze breaks out into a spontaneous applause. "Bravo, bravissimo, Wiley. Good show. I've always been impressed with how quickly you pounce onto your victims." She bleeds a dark smile my way before shooting those icy lasers she sees the world through back on her ex. "Lottie and Noah aren't married. They're cohabitating. Lottie is married to *Everett*."

Wiley blinks back and looks honestly thrown for a loop. Something tells me that's not easy to do with a con man of his caliber.

"Son"—he bounces his head toward Noah, agog—"is this true?"

Noah closes his eyes a moment. "True as the badge I've got in my pocket."

I lean in. "And the weapon strapped to his back." I thought I'd remind Wiley that Noah has bullets, and he's not afraid to use them. Since Noah was coming with me tonight, I didn't bother bringing Ethel. And now that I see how riled up I am, it's probably a very good thing.

Wiley gives a long blink himself. "So, what happened?" He shakes his head my way. "Why'd you leave Everett for Noah? If I remember correctly, women usually do it the other way around."

I'm pretty sure that's reference to Cormack and bitter days gone by. But per usual, Wiley has things all mixed up. Cormack left Everett for Noah.

Suze pumps out a devilish grin. "Lottie did it for the money. Everett came of age and received his inheritance in full, now that he's met the obligation of having a wife."

Wiley's mouth falls open. "You did it for money? Why, you're a woman after my own heart after all."

Good Lord up in heaven.

I shrug over at my mother. "At least he's honest."

Noah groans, "Dad, Lottie and I are together. Her marriage to Everett is in name only. She's the woman I've given my whole heart to. I want to spend the rest of my life with her."

"*Aw!*" Mom coos so loud a ten table radius cranes their necks this way.

Wiley chuckles. "That's what you said about the last one, son. Let's hope this one sticks."

A bout of nausea rolls through me at the thought of Noah making such a proclamation about Britney. Sure, they were married so he must have loved her, but a part of me wants to believe what Noah and I share is a first for both of us.

Everett bounces through my mind and I bounce him right back out.

Noah leans in, looking fit to kill. "This one is sticking." He looks from his father to his mother. "Both of you behave."

The waitress comes by, takes our order, and in a flash we're served our meals. Mom, Suze, and I opted for various versions of poultry, and the boys indulge in juicy steaks that are bloody enough to moo.

Mom leans her shoulder next to Wiley's. "Tell me about your future plans. How long do you think you'll be in Honey Hollow?"

He pats his lips with a napkin. "As long as you'll have me, darlin'."

Wow, he's so cheesy. Certainly my mother will see right through this Swiss cheese parade.

Mom giggles up a storm as if she were just asked out by the star quarterback—of a very dysfunctional team.

Okay, so maybe things aren't as transparent to her as they are to the rest of us.

Suze grunts, "And what about employment? Who's going to keep you in steaks?"

Wiley wraps an arm around my mother—again with the honesty.

"This pretty little lady right here offered me a prime position at the B&B—head bartender. I've even got a side gig lined up at the Evergreen, working special events. I'll be the senior mixologist at the Love at the Evergreen dance this Valentine's Day. And love will most certainly be in the air." He makes moony eyes at my mother and I openly gag.

"Love?" Suze balks. "You wouldn't know love if it bit you."

Wiley's gaze drifts to my mother. "She's bit me again and again, and I know it well. Believe me, I've got the bite marks to prove it."

Noah and I groan in unison.

Noah leans in, sighing with defeat as he tucks his lips close to my ear. "Why did Everett think this was a good idea again?"

"Maybe he was testing us," I whisper back.

Noah slumps back in his seat. "Testing my sanity is more like it."

Dinner goes on with Suze taking potshots at my mother and me, with Noah trying to get her to knock it off, and with Wiley all but biting my mother. Just when I'm about to cry uncle and run away with Noah, a couple enjoying their meal across the room catches my eye.

My mouth falls open, and I lean over to Noah. "Hey, isn't that Jodie McCloud?"

Noah's eyes dart across the room and he sits up straight. "Sure is."

The dark-haired gentleman sitting next to her looks vaguely familiar and I can't seem to pinpoint why. And then, like a thunderbolt, it hits me.

"Oh my goodness, I have to go to the little girls' room right this minute." I jump out of my seat without running my true intentions by Noah—mostly because I don't want to give him the opportunity to veto them.

I start to take off and Suze pulls me back.

"The bathroom is in the other direction." She tries spinning me around, and I jump from her grasp.

"I prefer going the long way. You know, work off the fried chicken." I bolt before another Fox can grab me in their clutches, namely Noah. It's bad enough I can feel his heated gaze burning a hole right through my back.

I thread my way through furniture and bodies until I come upon the small table in the back where Jodie and the dark-haired man from the community center sit. It's the same man that Whitney started to introduce me to but was cut off abruptly. I think she said his name was Ian something or other—or maybe she never got to the last name because Crystal Mandrake was quick to cut her off.

A couple from the dance floor gets a little too close to me and I go with it, bumping right into the cozy table set for two and sending their waters sloshing.

"Oh my goodness!" I say, picking up a spare napkin and dabbing the tablecloth. "I'm so sorry. It's just so crowded in here, and I think I got lost on my way to the restroom."

"Lottie?" Jodie looks up, wide-eyed, as her mouth rounds out with delight. She, too, has donned a red dress for the evening, and I'm beginning to feel as if I'm in some bizarre cult where they require you to wear the heated hue. Her auburn hair is loose and wavy, softening her features as it drapes to the side. Her lips are painted to match her dress, and it looks to be clear this is far more than some acquaintance she's meeting up with. This is a romantic dinner if ever there was one. "Lottie Lemon! What a small world. Fancy meeting you here."

A laugh gets caught in my throat as I feign surprise. "Jodie? This is too funny! I was just here with my boyfriend and his parents." I roll my eyes at the thought—and it's a one hundred percent genuine response on my part. "Sorry, I don't mean to be rude."

Jodie belts out a warm laugh. "Don't even worry about it. And don't get me started on my ex and his out-laws. I know exactly how complicated relationships can be." She settles her eyes on the man seated across from her.

I glance his way and force myself to do a double take at the dark-haired man with a lantern jaw and large dark eyes. He's lanky but fit, sinewy like a bicyclist, and there's an Irish charm about him in general.

"Oh hey!" I offer up a side of enthusiasm to go with his steak. "I think we met that night at the community center. Whitney introduced us. Or at least she started to. I'm Lottie Lemon. Jodie and I are competing in the Vermont's Best Baker competition together. Was it *Ethan*?" I don't want to seem too eager by actually spouting his name off.

"Ian." He nods. His smile is scant and his eyes look hard. It's clear I'm interrupting something.

"*Ian*." I snap my fingers. "That's right. It's nice to meet you more formally." I sober up quickly. "It's terrible what happened that night. Any thoughts on who could have done such a thing?"

Ian glances to Jodie. "I'd like to think it was an act of senseless violence. A robbery gone wrong, perhaps." He shrugs. "I just hope they catch the killer. My clients are running scared. They're worried he's targeting the bakers in the upcoming competition."

A chill runs through me as those nefarious cookie-based threats run through my mind.

"Clients?" I shake my head. "Can I ask what line of work you're in?"

"Nothing exciting," he muses.

Jodie scoffs. "You got that right." She glances up at me. "Ian is a walking, talking sweater." She gives a playful wink. "He's an accountant."

"Oh"—I look his way—"it must be your busy season."

"That it is." He tips his head as if I hit it right on the nose.

"Is that how you knew Whitney?" I couldn't help but ask. There has to be a connection someplace. She's the one that introduced us.

He glances to the crowd of bodies swaying on the dance floor.

"That's how I knew her. She was one of my first bakeries. I do most of the restaurants between here and Ashford."

"Wow, then you must really be busy." A thought comes to me. "Hey, if you've got room for one more, I'd love to talk to you some time. The accounting is all a bit overwhelming for me. I'd much rather focus on the baking."

He shakes his head before I can finish my last sentence. "I'm afraid I'm swamped. I can't take on another client even if I wanted to. I do have great colleagues, though. I can give your name out if you like."

A pink film glides over his shoulders, and I make a face at Taffy as he begins to appear.

Taffy hisses in his ear, "This is one genuine snake, Lottie. Book him." He gives a dark laugh. "Get it? He said he's an accountant. Snake? Book him?" He twitches his head my way. "Someone is playing hard to get with their sense of humor tonight. Did one of these ninnies kill my Patty Cakes?"

I shrug, mostly for Taffy's benefit. "That would be great. I'm over in Honey Hollow—the Cutie Pie Bakery and Cakery. I'm right on Main Street."

"Perfect." Ian picks up his knife and fork and positions it over his steak. "If anyone has an opening, I'll be sure to send them your way."

"Thank you. I'll let you get back to your dinner." I bite down on my lip as I look to Jodie. "Oh, since you're here—you wouldn't happen to know how I could get in touch with Larissa Miller, would you? I tried to call the competition to let them know I have a couple of questions. I've got a winning cookie recipe, but the dough has to be refrigerated overnight. But they said she recently changed her number. I thought maybe I'd pop in and find her at work. Time is running out and I need to perfect my recipes."

Her lips pull down. "I'm pretty sure they won't allow dough being brought in. You're wise to ask." She glances to the ceiling. "You know, I think she mentioned once something about the Lakehouse Inn."

"The one in Fallbrook?" I inch back. "That's fancy."

Ian nods as he chews down a bite. "It's also closed."

"That's too bad." Darn it. "Maybe it was too pricey for its own good. Rumor had it, you needed to mortgage your home to eat a meal there." Or in my case, give up your rent money. "Any clue where she's at now?" I direct the question to Jodie.

She twists her lips. "No, but good luck to you. I'd have another recipe on hand if I were you."

"Good thinking. Enjoy your dinner."

I'm about to make my way back when I bump into a body, and the next thing I know I'm in the thick of the dance floor swaying to the music, safe in Noah Fox's strong and capable arms.

"Lottie"—he sighs heated into my ear—"I never let you out of my sight."

"That's just the way I like it." A giggle gets locked in my throat just as I spot my mother and Wiley doing this exact same thing and my mood quickly sours.

"What did you glean?" Noah leans back and traps my gaze with those evergreen eyes.

"You'll have to drag it out of me in a far more creative manner, Detective."

"Oh? Prepare yourself. You're about to be detained for questioning." He dots a kiss to my cheek. "All night long."

"As long as you end each question with a kiss, I just might cooperate."

"I have far more carnal ways of getting you to speak," he whispers the words hot right into my ear and my insides squeeze tight at the naughty proposition.

Mom bursts into a fit of giggles and howls, prompting both Noah and me to glance their way, only to find Wiley, the vampire, has struck again.

"I think he's out for blood," I muse. "You don't really think he'd bilk her out of her money, do you? Believe me, my mother is far more interested in giving up bodily fluids."

"Blood would be cheaper." Noah's dimples invert. "But if I know my old man, he still likes to cash out while he's ahead. We'll have to keep an eye out on those two."

I grimace at the thought. "Noah, can you believe my mother—and your father?"

He closes his eyes and shakes his head. "Lord have mercy on us all."

"But, on an up note, none of my mother's relationships as of late seem to last."

Noah tips his head to the side. "Come to think of it, my father likes to cap things off early himself."

"Here's hoping this will be a short and sweet ride without any financial casualties along the way."

"Lottie, I can promise you that man is not taking off with your mother's money. I'll handcuff him and haul him down to the Ashford Sheriff's Department myself if a dime goes missing from the B&B."

I offer up a crooked grin to the handsome detective before me. "How about you practice using those handcuffs in just a few hours?"

"I have been meaning to arrest a certain baker for stealing my heart."

A quiet laugh pumps through me. At least he didn't add the fact that I stomped on it. I would never mean to hurt Noah intentionally.

"I was thinking more along the lines of handcuffing Carlotta to her room, but your idea sounds a lot more interesting."

Carlotta walked in on Noah and me twice last night and almost used my vanity as a toilet. Apparently, she's got a quasi-sleepwalking situation going on—or so she says. I'm thinking she just wanted a peek at a drop-dead gorgeous, very much naked detective—and believe me when I say she got an eyeful. She apologized profusely after I screamed at the top of my lungs and instructed Noah to shoot on sight.

And she also politely offered to lock the door behind her—which as evidenced by her second entry later that night, she did no such thing.

Noah bucks with a laugh. "I might have another set in the truck."

"I knew I liked you."

Noah sobers up. "I know I love you." He lands a careful kiss over my lips and incinerates me from the inside. Noah kisses me senseless right here on the dance floor, our bodies moving in time to the rhythm of our hearts. His lips roam over to my ear as he buries a kiss over my temple. "I can't bear the thought of anything happening to you. Steer clear of this case, Lottie. It's a dangerous one. Do it for me. I'm begging you."

Noah is begging me to steer clear.

It's a dangerous case.

Double homicide.

Blatant threats to my own safety.

There's a killer out there.

A stalker.

A couple of parents with far too many hormones to contend with.

It's as if the world has gone haywire.

My lips form to assure Noah that I will do exactly as he's requested of me, but the words refuse to come.

Instead, I offer a circular nod that says nothing and everything at once.

Noah sighs as he closes his eyes. He's acquiescing to what he knows to be true.

There's a killer out there, and I'm determined to find them.

Larissa Miller—you're next on my suspect list.

Let's hope you have a good alibi.

You're going to need it.

10

The next day is spent in a frenzy as the bakery sells out of those iced conversation heart sugar cookies at a frenetic speed.

"I've never seen anything like it," Lily laments as the rush dies down well after four in the afternoon. "We've been going full steam since seven this morning. What gives?"

"I don't know, but almost all of them said they came from the Haunted Honey Hollow Tour at my mother's B&B. Maybe she's running a special today?"

"Well, tell her to warn you next time, or I might be moved to kill and she just might be the one haunting her B&B." Lily glowers at the mess left in the kitchen.

We've got icing and cookies just about everywhere—and some of that is the fault of a couple of hungry ghosts. Once Princess and Taffy figured out they could eat as much as they wanted, they quickly dived into the deep end of the icing tub.

I'm not sure if there are any sanitary issues with that, but as far as I can tell the only damage done was to the psyche of the kitchen staff.

"I'll text my mother and see what's going on."

No sooner do I shoot her a text than she walks right through the door like the apparition Lily is determined to make her. She's donned a hot pink wool coat and has a scarf, gloves, and handbag to match. If Miranda Lemon is anything, she's forever a walking runway.

"Miranda Lemon," Lily snaps. "You have no idea what cookie carnage you just caused at the bakery."

Mom chortles as she covers her mouth. "You're welcome, ladies." She gives a cheeky wink. "It was all Wiley's idea. The man is brilliant, I tell you."

I lean my ear her way, filled with suspicion. "What exactly was his idea?"

Mom pulls her shocking pink coat tight around her as if she were giddy with excitement.

"Wiley had me hike the price of the B&B tours up by twenty dollars and offer a free cocktail and free cookies. We had three times the tourists head our way. The price bump more than paid for the liquor and Wiley made a ton of money just in tips!"

My mouth falls open. "Mother, that's—" I blow out a breath. "Okay, fine, that is pretty genius. But you do realize that I don't charge you for the cookies I send to the B&B."

"Which brings me to my next point." She swats the counter with her gloves. "I'll need twice as many of those cute conversation heart cookies for tomorrow."

I scoff without meaning to. "You're letting them eat cookies? I'm shocked they're coming this way at all. I'm pretty sure I'm getting the losing end of the stick here."

Lily shakes her head. "I'm not sure about that, Lot. All you have to do is raise your prices a notch. Every one of those people were buying boxes full of them to take back home. I heard a couple people saying they were addicted and couldn't get enough."

"You have a point," I say. "Keep up the good work, Mother." Another small crowd comes in and Lily heads off to tend to them. "So how did things end with Wiley last night? Should I be afraid to ask?"

Her lips twist to the side, assuring me I should have feared for my sanity before tossing the question out there.

"A girl never kisses and tells." She wrinkles her nose. "But he's still playing hard to get. Do you think there's something wrong with him? Worse yet, do you think there's something wrong with *me*?"

A flood of relief hits me. "Maybe he still has a spark for Suze? You know they were married for a very long time."

Mom is quick to wave it off. "Suze couldn't care less if Wiley was eaten by a pack of wolves. She told him so herself before we left the restaurant." She makes a face. "I've never been so rebuffed by a man. It's an incredible turn-on."

A moan evicts from me. "Could you refrain from using those words in the salacious sense? There are some things I don't care to know about. But I am sorry you're feeling rejected. That's not a good thing. In fact, I say you teach him a lesson and find yourself another man to glom onto. Preferably someone sane who has never faked his own death before."

She sags at the thought. "You and I both know that's like looking for a needle in a haystack." She motions to the heart-shaped red velvet cake in the window, frosted with cream cheese and garnished with fresh strawberries to accentuate its loveable shape. "I'll take that, Lottie. If I can't get in through his libido, I'll get in through his stomach. That man will be mine by Valentine's Day. Just you wait and see."

"That's what I'm afraid of."

Lily comes over and boxes it up for her. "If it were only that easy to snag a man, Miranda," she muses. "On second thought, Lottie, I'm putting in an order for a cake just like it. I think I know what I'm giving Alex for Valentine's Day."

"Cake is one of the best gifts," I say. "And no one ever turns down my red velvet."

Lily shakes her head. "I'm giving him myself with a giant red bow on my naked body. The cake is just a snack for later."

"I thought this was Naomi's month?"

She shrugs. "Rumor has it, there's a new girl in town and she's coming after Alex hard. They've already gone to coffee twice. For Alex that's as good as an engagement."

I suck in a quick breath. "It's not that Serena Digby woman, is it?"

Lily nods. "And rumor also has it, she's a bona fide witch. I bet she drugged him with some real life love potion."

I avert my eyes at the thought. "Please, if she had a love potion that really worked, both Cormack and Cressida would have poisoned Noah and Everett by now."

Mom pulls out her phone and begins pecking away. "How do you spell Digby?"

"Never you mind," I say.

Mom takes the pastry box filled with heart-shaped intentions and speeds off for the B&B with a hasty farewell.

"Lily, do you know anything about the old Lakehouse Inn?" I ask.

"The one in Fallbrook?" She pulls out her phone and wrestles it out with Google. "Closed last year about this time. It was owned by the head chef, a man by the name of Leslie Aaronson."

"That's a unique name." I pull out my own phone and quickly look him up. "Check this out. He opened a new restaurant in Oklahoma called Blue Sky. I wonder if he's there now?" I hit the call button next to the restaurant's info.

A friendly woman picks up, and as soon as I ask to speak with Leslie, I'm put on hold. A moment later, an equally friendly male answers the phone.

I do a quick introduction and let him know I'm looking for my friend, Larissa Miller.

He gives a dark chuckle. "Friend, huh? You don't need to beat around the deadbeat bush with me. She owes you money, doesn't she?"

A breath hitches in my throat.

She owes people money? Is that what he remembers about her?

I decide to go with it.

"You called it. I really just want to touch base with her one more time. You know, try to see if I could squeeze some blood from that turnip."

He chuckles again. "Larissa has her problems, but she's a good person at heart. She was desperate when I closed the restaurant. I heard she went to work at Patisserie, and when she's not there, she's at Diamonds working her other gig."

"Diamonds?" The place doesn't ring a bell. "What's her other gig?"

"Waitress. She worked nights at Diamonds when she worked for me as well."

"I wonder why she has to work two jobs?" And borrow money from people on the side.

"Never asked. Drugs, alcohol, dying father, who knows? Larissa was harder to penetrate than Fort Knox. Good luck with getting your dough. She's notorious for getting away with murder."

My blood runs cold when he says it.

We quickly hang up and I look up Diamonds without missing a beat. I shake my head at what I find.

I put in a text to both Noah and Everett separately and ask if they've got plans tonight.

Noah texts back. **Cormack just dropped by the precinct with milkshakes as a peace offering. She's apologizing for her crass behavior for the past few months. By the way, the milkshake made me crave you more. But I might have a break in the case. I'll be home late. Stay safe. Love you.**

Everett texts back. **Cressida just stopped by the courthouse with coffee. She says she wanted to apologize for the way she's been behaving. Just FYI, your coffee is better. This was bitter to the last drop.**

Well, isn't that something? It looks as if Honey Hollow's resident witch has been brewing up a cauldron of deceit and hocking it to two blonde bimbos that I'm betting aren't sorry about anything.

Love potion.

More like digestive issues in the making. But considering the fact neither of them has dropped dead, I decide to push the potion issue aside for now.

I do a little digging, and it turns out Diamonds is in the most dicey corner that Leeds has to offer. I'd hate to go there alone.

Princess and Taffy float out of the kitchen, moaning and looking bloated if that were at all possible.

"Heaven help us." Princess croaks the words out. "You'll have to find the killer soon, Lottie, before I die all over again. In fact, I plan on smothering myself with sugary pleasure each and every day until I do just that."

Taffy hisses my way, "She's not talking about the sweets in your kitchen, Lottie. Word on the supernatural street is, Thirteen has gone into hiding."

Princess swipes a lazy paw his way. "He has not. He's gearing up for our next date. He said something about a romantic rendezvous in the alley behind the B&B that involves spaghetti. It's inspired by something he saw in a movie once. I just can't wait to get sweaty in the spaghetti with him."

I sigh at the romantic implications of it all. "Love really is in the air. February sure knows how to bring out the good, the witchy, and the sweaty when it comes to that four letter word." A thought comes to me. "The sooner we can land that killer behind bars, the sooner I can focus on my own love life."

I dig Ethel out of my ground safe, ask Lily to close up shop for me, and head out to Leeds myself with a sexed-up kitten and an ornery snake.

"You don't need a man, Lottie." Princess sniffs after I tell her all about the Noah and Everett poison potion debacle. "Now pick up your pace. We need to get to Diamonds before all the good ones are taken. With a name like that, every kitten in Vermont will be clawing to get through the door."

Taffy hisses as he slithers his way across my shoulders. "Lottie doesn't need a man to give her diamonds. She's rich with frosting and cookies. She already has everything a girl could ask for. Trust me, Princess. She'll never need a man again. She's a modern independent woman who knows that real happiness lies at the bottom of a tub of icing."

I shrug his way. "I can't quite fight you on it. Let's hope being independent doesn't prove to be a real killer."

Heigh-ho, heigh-ho—it's off to Leeds we go.

11

Diamonds Diner Club sits along a row of relatively decent looking establishments, which is actually a pleasant surprise as far as Leeds goes. Geographically, Leeds sits just below Honey Hollow and is home to most every seedy and greedy establishment you can think of. Although, I'll admit, with all the snow we've been getting, even Leeds looks as if it's out of a storybook sprinkled with frosty magic.

The exterior of the Diamonds Diner Club is painted silver, and if my eyes aren't deceiving me, it's covered with a glittering effect as well. A large sign spikes into the night, depicting a woman in a hot pink gown, dripping with diamonds that assures me I've arrived at my destination.

No sooner do I find a spot in the parking lot out back than my phone bleats. It's a text from Everett.

Leeds? Lemon, you know it's dangerous there. Do you have Ethel with you?

I cringe at the phone. "It's Everett," I say to Princess and Taffy. "He wants to know if I have my gun."

I text right back. **Wait a minute—you're having me followed! It's that wall of muscles you hired to sit around my bakery all day, isn't it?**

My phone bleats again. **Just talked to Seven. Be there in less than ten minutes. I'd ask you to stay in your car, but I know better. I'll meet you inside. Stay out of trouble.**

"Seven?" I say, glancing around until I spot that same black Mustang that's been parked in front of my shop for the last week solid. "Apparently, that's the name of the muscle man who's been keeping an eye on me. What kind of a person goes through life as a number?"

Princess purrs as if partaking in the greatest pleasure. "The kind of man who has two lives to go. Sounds like Seven enjoys a bit of danger. I've been keeping an eye out on him, and I do approve of every one of those muscles."

"Ignore her, Lottie," Taffy grunts. "She's got a thing for men who have numbers for names. Let's get inside so I can find a glass of water to douse her with. It's clear this Seven person wants to keep his anonymity."

"Don't worry, Taffy. I plan on giving it to him." I collect my purse and both Taffy and Princess float along as we walk the shoveled path that leads to the front.

Inside of Diamonds, it's warm, toasty even. There's a reception area where they check my coat, and after examining the other patrons, I quickly realize I'm sorely underdressed.

"Oh, Lottie!" Princess scampers forward and cranes her neck into the main seating area. "Everyone is so beautiful. I want to live here. Surely, this is where I've been destined to be all along. My Whitney would have loved it here. She had a penchant for luxury."

"And judges," I say. But I couldn't help the quip. Apparently, Whitney and Everett spent many a summers together in the lap of luxury. I guess I can't fault them for how they grew up, but it doesn't mean I have to like the idea of them summering in the same bed.

A tall woman with dark, wavy hair, delicately pointed nose, almond-shaped eyes, and an all-around familiarity about her steps up and gasps when she sees me.

It's Larissa Miller.

Oh dear Lord, the last thing I expected was to bump into her so quickly.

"Lottie Lemon." Her shoulders pull back as she tips her chin up. "I guess my secret is out." She gives a little wink. "I work here, evenings." She shrugs as if she were indifferent to it. "Some of us need all the cash we can get our hands on."

A light laugh strums from me. "That would be all of us."

Taffy slithers over my shoulders, and I can feel his heft. Larissa's eyes widen as she seemingly looks his way.

Taffy jerks his head up. "I think she sees me."

Larissa gives a quick blink, and her eyes meet with mine. "I'll be your waitress tonight. Are you meeting someone here?" She points to the grand dining room behind her.

"Yes, actually. But I'm the first to arrive. A table for two will be perfect."

"Sure thing." She motions for me to follow as she navigates us into a gorgeous dimly lit room with white walls that sparkle and shimmer. Bistro tables are set out, each one draped in a black cloth with a candle dotting the center. There's a dance floor and a large prominent bar, and the sound of classical music flows from the speakers. But it's the men and women who populate this place that deserve an honorable mention. Each one of them is dressed to the nines—the women in cocktail dresses and the men in dark suits.

We're about to pass a well-coifed couple when I take a better look at the blonde before me and I stop dead in my tracks.

"*Aspen?*"

Aspen Nash is one of my three half-siblings. She's a blonde version of Betty Boop with her sassy shoulder-length bob, her big pouty lips, and heavily drawn-in eyes. She's got that va-va-voom figure and a black velvet dress that intends on showing every inch of it off.

"Lottie?" She squints as she leans forward. Taffy hisses her way. I'm guessing that's his go-to greeting. "Hey!" She glances to her date, an older gentleman who looks as if he could be her grandfather, and Princess is quick to hop in his lap.

The coitally prone kitten purrs. "Ooh, he's nice, Lottie. Can we keep him? Can we?" I shake my head over at her just enough to get my point across. He's on the phone chatting away, so Aspen stands and offers me a quick embrace.

Her mouth rounds out with surprise. "Are you working the floor tonight, too?"

"*What*?" I lean back and spot Larissa at a vacant table patiently waiting for me. "No, I'm meeting Everett for dinner."

Princess hops up on the table. "Ooh, Everett for dinner. Now there's a meal I wouldn't mind sinking my teeth into."

Heaven help me.

I turn my body just enough to where I'm giving Aspen my full attention.

Aspen cocks her head to the side. "Dinner, huh? I guess you don't know. Diamonds is a virtual playground for the Elite Entourage."

I gasp as I do a quick inventory of its patrons with a whole new set of eyes. The Elite Entourage is basically a high-class call girl service. I happen to know that not only do both of my half-sisters, Aspen and Kelleth, participate in the perverse organization but so does Keelie's sister, Naomi. And each one of them swears they're not doing the hanky panky—they're simply traipsing all the way to the bank in their sparkly high heels.

Aspen glowers. "And before you get judgmental, I'm only keeping the men company. I look at it as dinner and a bonus." She hitches her brows playfully. "I better get back." She points to her date who just put his phone into his pocket. "Kelleth is here somewhere, too. I'll talk to you later."

"For sure," I say as I quickly catch up to Larissa. "That was my half-sister." I shrug up at her and her mouth falls open.

"You're related to Aspen and Kelleth?" Larissa looks stymied by this as she lands a couple of menus down onto the table.

I nod over at her. "I just found out not too long ago."

Larissa cocks her head to the side. "And you know why they're here?"

Taffy slithers into my peripheral vision. "And I have a feeling we know why our suspect is here as well."

I shoot the wily snake a quick look before reverting my attention to Larissa. "You mean, do I know they belong to the EE, aka the Elite Entourage? Unfortunately." My fingers quickly fly to my lips in the event the staff is in on the naughty gig themselves. "Not that I'm judging. Hey, if that's what you're comfortable with, I've got no problem with it."

"Me?" Larissa digs a finger into her chest and laughs. "Oh heavens, not me, Lottie. Not that I haven't considered it." She chuckles as if she were joking. "That would be the Samson option. Right now I'm keeping my head above water—just barely. And believe me when I say I've resorted to dicey measures, but I guess you could say I haven't hit rock bottom yet." She blinks back. "I'm sorry. You're not a part of the EE, are you?"

A quick laugh percolates from me. "No. Definitely not. I guess my date and I chose the wrong establishment."

"You didn't if he's a good tipper. That's exactly why I'm here. These sugar daddies, as they call them, are generous to a fault. I could pay my rent alone off my tips. Personally, I think the reason they tip so much is to impress the dates they purchase." She averts her eyes. "Not that I care what their motives are. And don't worry about the place. Every now and again we get nice people like you. The food is great here and so is the ambience. So long as your date doesn't have a wandering eye, you should be good to go. We seem to have an abundance of attractive ladies. Oh, and word to the wise, the EE has about three of these stomping grounds. I'd check with your sisters if you didn't want to get caught up in this nonsense."

"Thanks for the heads-up."

Larissa heads off and I take a seat as Taffy slithers out onto the table before me.

"We need to question her, Lottie. Patricia is dead. And if I find out that woman had anything to do with it, I'll make sure she ends up that way, too." He hisses each word out like the threat it was meant to be.

I give a quick glance around as I lean in. "That's not how this works. We solve the case and that's it. The law takes it from there, and the two of you get whisked off to paradise. You're welcome." I blink a quick smile as Princess hops to the other side of the table.

"Ignore him, Lottie," she mewls. "He was born and bred to kill. He just wants the homicidal spotlight to himself."

Taffy lifts his head in the air in a threatening manner. "Ignore *her*, Lottie. She was born and bred to breed, thus the constant yearning for attention."

Before I say a thing, a tall, dark, and vexingly handsome judge falls in the seat across from me.

"Lemon." Everett's lids hood low and his lips curve just enough as he reaches over and kisses the back of my hand. "You look exquisite."

"You do realize I'm the only girl here in jeans and a sweater."

"The right jeans and the right sweater on the right girl. Now, why isn't Noah here with you?"

"Because he thinks it's too dangerous for me to be anywhere apparently—thus he wouldn't have let me come. And don't play innocent. I happen to know you feel the same."

His lids hood another notch. "That's because it's true."

I lean in. "Are you really having that wall of muscles—Seven follow me everywhere I go? *Everywhere*?"

"Everywhere."

"Well then." I lean back in my seat, more than slightly incensed. "I guess I'll have to check my shower curtain at night before I use the restroom."

His lips twitch. "How's it going with Carlotta? Any more hot wax incidences?"

I make a face. "If there are, I don't want to know about it. Speaking of things I don't want to know about..." I lean in and tell him about the nefarious underpinnings about this place.

Everett scours the vicinity. "I knew that, Lemon."

"What?"

"Yup. It's not uncommon for the girls who work in the EE to filter through the judicial system. They've named the place before."

I suck in a quick breath. "Everett, this can't be good for your reputation."

"It's fine. I'm here with my wife, remember?"

Princess moans as she pretends to faint. "Lottie, he's perfect. Just *purrfect*! Oh, take him home right this minute. I'm sure Carlotta will share her hot wax with you. I can't take the heat from this man. I just can't take it."

Everett's chest bounces with a laugh, and it's only then I note we're still holding hands.

Taffy coils his body around the votive candle in the middle of the table. "Wake me when this nightmare is over, would you?"

Everett nods past me and I turn to see Larissa talking to a tall, dark, and handsome homicide detective before leading him this way.

She giggles as she seats him. "Two dates, Lottie? I think you could teach every one of the girls here a lesson."

I wrinkle my nose at the thought. "Something tells me some of the girls here are far too familiar with having to handle two men."

Larissa laughs as she takes off.

But I'm not laughing. In fact, I'm not all that happy with the two men before me.

"You both realize I could have questioned her far more efficiently on my own."

Noah tips his head to the side. "You do realize that you could have gotten killed on your own as well the night of the murders, or any other night that's since followed."

161

Everett's brows peak. "You're being stalked all on your own as well."

"Fine." I wave them off. "What's new with the case, Noah? Any leads on who could have done this?"

Noah's eyes flit in the direction Larissa took off in. "After you told me about the fact both Jodie and Ruthie claimed to see Larissa speaking to Patricia and Whitney, I decided to seize the security tapes from their bakeries."

"You did?" I scoot my chair close to his and Princess wedges her fluffy self between us.

"Knowledge is such an aphrodisiac, Lottie," she purrs. "I bet Carlotta has enough hot wax to go around. Let's invite the dashing detective to the after-party as well. You know what they say—two's company, three's a night to remember."

My lips twist to the side as I shoot the pesky poltergeist a look.

"Go on, Noah," I say.

Noah glances to both Everett and me. "Two days before the murders, Larissa was seen paying a visit to both bakeries. She had what looked to be a tense conversation with both Whitney and Patricia in a private area—and it looks as if both women slipped her some cash."

"What?" I squawk so loud half the restaurant turns our way for a moment, and I hold my breath until the attention subsides. "Oh my goodness, Noah. Do you think she was taking bribes to influence the contest? And if so, why not hit up all the bakers?"

Noah shakes his head. "I don't know. And I don't know why she took the money. We're still investigating. So I would appreciate it if you went easy on any questions you might have for her."

"Scandalous," I say.

Everett takes a breath. "Something like this isn't only scandalous, it's illegal."

I bite down on my lower lip as I glance her way. "But is it motive for murder?"

Larissa comes back and we order dinner and drinks. Everett and Noah actually have a real conversation about police procedurals and something to do with budget cuts down at the precinct. Just as their conversation wanders off into sports, I excuse myself for the restroom.

Taffy glides over my shoulders for the ride.

"We're not headed to the loo, are we, Lottie?"

"Maybe, maybe not. But first, there's a certain suspect I'd like to question a little further."

I head to the foyer and Larissa spots me.

"Can I help you, Lottie?" She offers an affable smile.

"Just looking for the restroom."

"To your right. If anyone asks for a recommendation, just say no. The girls are forever going in there exchanging info on their dates." Her gaze darts to the ceiling.

"I will. Can I ask if everything's still on for the Vermont's Best Baker competition? I mean, two bakers were taken out pretty brutally."

Her chest depresses with a sigh. "I know it. Isn't it horrible? I can't imagine why anyone would want those girls dead."

Taffy rears his head and hisses at her as if he were about to strike and Larissa jumps a good foot back.

My mouth falls open as does hers, and her eyes are wide with fright as she looks to me.

"Oh my goodness," I whisper. "You can see him."

She shakes her head just barely. "I don't know what you're talking about." She takes a quick breath and composes herself in an instant. Gone is the frazzled exterior and it's quickly replaced with the rigid bravado she's known for. "If you're speculating the killer is a man, I would have to agree with you. Women don't typically resort to such violence."

I shrug a little. "Unless it was a hit." I decide to go along with it for now. "You know, maybe either Whitney and Patricia made someone angry—maybe they owed someone *money*."

Her left cheek flinches as if I struck her.

"I guess anything is possible." She swallows hard. "The competition is still on, Lottie. We look forward to seeing what you'll bring to the table."

My shoulders sag and Taffy nearly slides right off. "Larissa, is there anything at all you could think of that might have been suspicious the night of the murders? Whitney and Patricia were warring it out over cookies. But someone else did this to them. I've racked my brain for any idea of what might have gone wrong, but I can't figure it out. I'd sure sleep better if I knew."

She glances to Taffy briefly before looking me in the eye. "You and me both."

My heart thumps wildly because I'm almost certain Larissa is supersensual—unless, of course, my powers are growing, and in doing so giving the rest of the world an opportunity to see the dead as well. Now that would be a disastrously deadly plot twist I have no desire to see come to fruition.

Larissa leans in. "I did see Whitney talking to a dark-haired man. They looked as if they were having a heated discussion about something." She shrugs. "I spotted the same man talking to Patricia as well."

That night comes back in snatches. As soon as I came in, I spotted a man with his arms around both their shoulders before taking off and speaking to the other contestants. They sure looked chummy. A thought comes to me.

"Was that Ian Gardner?" I ask. "The accountant?"

She snaps her fingers at me. "That's the guy. I guess a bunch of bakers use him." She shrugs. "He seemed sweet, though. I didn't get any dark vibes about him. I'm generally able to read people pretty well."

"What did you think of Whitney and Patricia?"

Larissa takes a deep breath, her eyes set to some invisible horizon.

"Whitney was a bit uptight, but she warmed up to me eventually. Patricia was goal-oriented, I'll give her that."

Warmed up? Goal-oriented? Something tells me Larissa here was an expert at shaking them both down. But why?

I clear my throat. "I hope you don't think it's crass of me to ask, but why the two jobs? I know you're a celebrated pastry chef."

She closes her eyes briefly. "If I told you, I'm afraid you'd think it were ridiculous and unbelievable." She gives a sorrowful chuckle. "Come to think of it, my entire life as of late has become quite unbelievable and not in any good way." She nods to the kitchen. "I'd better get back to work." She glances at Taffy before dragging her eyes slowly to mine. "I'll be by your table shortly to see about dessert."

She takes off and Taffy hisses, "She looked right at me, Lottie. She can see the dead."

"Let's just pray it's not a catching condition."

Everett, Noah, and I finish up our meal. Larissa brings us a complimentary slice of chocolate cake, and the three of us split it before we head back to Honey Hollow.

But my mind is reeling with two red-hot questions. Is Larissa Miller supersensual? And worse yet, is she a killer?

I'm pretty certain she was accepting bribes from Whitney and Patricia.

But why?

There's only one way to find out. And I'm pretty sure Noah and Everett won't like it.

12

The snow sifts softly over Honey Hollow, covering the trees, the rooftops, and every inch of the ground in a blanket of white.

It's the middle of the afternoon, and the Cutie Pie Bakery and Cakery just finished another rush of tourists, all clamoring for my conversation heart sugar cookies.

Lily grunts as she refastens her apron, "Can you believe we actually had a request to write *RIP Whitney and Patricia* on a cookie?"

I make a face and nod. "People are twisted. Of course, I said no. But we sold out anyway. Good thing I've already whipped up a few more batches. I just need the cookies to cool so I can ice them."

Lily's attention strays to where that wall of muscles sits staring at his phone.

"He's watching a movie." Lily sighs. "Every now and again I head on over and spy on him. Are you sure his name is Seven?"

I shrug. "I told you that's what Everett said." Taffy's comment comes back to me. "I'm betting it's just a cover. Something tells me he wants to remain an enigma."

Lily licks her lips as she scours over him with her gaze.

"Hey?" A laugh bubbles to my lips. "You're interested in more than what he's watching. You think he's cute, don't you?"

"Eh." She shrugs "He's all right if you're into the tall, strong, and silent type. Don't forget irresistibly good looking. Just think of the things he could do with those big, beefy mitts he calls hands."

"All right, all right." I fan her with a kitchen towel. "Why don't you take him some sweet treats and see if you can get him to spill all his deep, dark secrets?"

"*Ooh,* good idea." She quickly loads up a plate with a couple of brownie tarts, a mini lava cake, and fudge bottom cupcakes. "I happen to know he's a chocoholic. Each time I offer him a treat, he only accepts the ones with chocolate." She takes off just as my mother and Carlotta glide into the shop. And I can't help but note that Taffy has draped himself over Carlotta's shoulders once again.

"Hello, ladies, what can I get the two of you?"

Mom frowns at the items on the bakery shelf. "Got any love potion lying around? I'm afraid it's what I'll have to resort to. Wiley is still keeping me at an arm's length."

Carlotta stretches her lips across her face. "You can thank your daughter for that. Or more to the point, *I* should thank your daughter for that. Wiley asked me out for drinks later."

"Don't you dare." Mom wags a finger at her. "Lottie, call off your men. I've got my sights set on a Wiley Fox and gosh darn I'm going to nab him, trap him, and strap him to my bed." She tips her nose my way. "My truth or dare affair is tomorrow night, and I'll need all the luscious desserts you can give me. Maybe you can ask Noah what kind of desserts his father likes? I'm really hoping we can turn a corner before the big day."

Carlotta grunts, "So V-Day is D-Day huh? What are the plans for the naughty night, anyway?"

Mom sniffs. "Wiley has already agreed to be my date at the Evergreen on Valentine's Day. It's just a matter of time that man succumbs to my advances. In fact, I've got a couples' scavenger hunt happening at the B&B on Saturday night, but what Wiley doesn't know is that we're the only two participating."

Carlotta honks out a laugh. "And I bet that last stop will be in your bedroom."

Mom takes in a quick breath. "You really are devious. I'd better make a note." She takes off for a seat and shakes her purse upside down until a pen and a pad of paper tumble out.

Carlotta leans in. "So who's on first? Taffy here says you think a transmundane gal did it."

I shoot the supernatural serpent a wry smile. "I didn't say that. But I think he nailed the transmundane thing. Hey, you don't think my powers are growing in the wrong direction, do you? Do you think regular people can now see the dead? I had Taffy wrapped around my neck last night just the way you do now."

"Here." She gifts him to me and he happily finds a home over my shoulders. "Hey, Miranda, get a load of this hickey on our baby girl's neck."

"What?" Mom squawks as she clip-clops over. "Where is it? More importantly, who gave you the delicious love bite?"

I roll my eyes. "That would be Noah. We're back together, sort of."

Carlotta waves her hand up and down Taffy while the salty snake does his best to snap and hiss at my mother.

Mom makes a face. "Tell him to try harder next time. I don't see a thing. I bet that judge could give him a few lessons." She traipses back to the table in an effort to put her purse back together again.

Carlotta shrugs. "That suspect of yours must be transmundane. And if she's seeing the dead, she's supersensual. I say you call her out on it."

"I'm not calling her out. I'm investigating her. Noah said she was doing some shady business at both the Sweet Sin Bakery and the Upper Crust Bake Shop two days before the big double homicide. It looks as if both Whitney and Patricia were caught on security footage giving her something. Patricia gave an envelope, and it looked as if Whitney gave her cash." I got those details out of Noah last night. Let the record show, I have my ways.

"So what are you going to do about it?"

"I think I'll ask the girls running the shops if they noticed they were short on cash that day. And then there's Crystal Mandrake's bakery—A Cake Above. I saw Larissa talking to Crystal, too, the day of the murders. I thought I'd dig around a little and see if they're missing cash as well."

"Good luck to you." She points down at a miniature cherry pie and I quickly accommodate her.

"Heavens," Taffy moans. "Don't waste time feeding Carlotta. You've got three bakeries to hit."

Carlotta grunts through a bite of cherry pie, "I'm riding shotgun."

"We can't go to Hollyhock, Fallbrook, and Ashford all in one afternoon." A thought hits me. "I'll be right back."

I head to my office and call both Jodie at Sweet Sin and Ruthie at the Upper Crust Bake Shop and let them know that I discovered a huge deficit on the second of February. I told them it seemed to be a running scam by a seedy customer, and that a lot of businesses were hit that day. Both Jodie and Ruthie said they'd get back to me on it.

I head out to the front just as Lily comes my way with an ear-to-ear grin on her face.

"His name is Miles Rock and he's from Leeds, born and raised." She practically squeals as she says it. Lily never squeals. This is disconcerting on many levels, but I push all of that aside for a moment.

"Really? He told you all that?"

"A little chocolate goes a long way. That and I pulled out all the stops with him." She wiggles her shoulders. "I had to. Alex has me thinking I've lost my touch, but Miles just proved me wrong. We're going to dinner as soon as I close up the shop. He says that's when Noah and Everett take over and start watching you."

I make a face. "You mean babysitting." I glance at my phone. "I'm going to run out to Ashford real quick. I'll be back in time to help you close."

"No." Lily stomps her foot as she whines. "That means Miles has to follow you."

"Well, look at it this way. It'll give him a chance to miss you."

"Good thinking! On second thought, take your time." She checks her face in the framed mirror behind me. "Stay out as long as you need to."

I say a quick goodbye to my mother, grab Carlotta, and we're on our way to Ashford to see my archnemesis in baking—Crystal Mandrake.

A Cake Above is located in a ritzy part of downtown Ashford sandwiched somewhat between the courthouse and the Ashford Sheriff's Department.

"You know"—I say to Carlotta, Taffy, and Princess who has decided to take a break from her feline boy toy, Thirteen—"had I thought it through, I could have opened my bakery right here in Ashford. Not only would I have been a guaranteed thorn in Crystal Mandrake's side, but I would have been spitting distance from Everett and Noah. Oh, who am I kidding? I'd never get any work done that way."

A Cake Above has its exterior windows covered with stickers that boast of all the competitions that Crystal has won. Right above the sign with the store's moniker there's a banner that reads *voted best bakery in Vermont five years in a row!*

Carlotta shakes her head at the wall of accolades. "At least she's humble."

"I'll say."

Taffy hisses, "Don't worry, Lottie. I rather enjoy wreaking havoc on those with inflated egos."

"I'll take a hard pass on the offer, Taffy. But thank you for thinking of me."

We head on in through the door while Princess and Taffy float their way in through the window and bypass the counter altogether as they head straight into the bakery shelves, and I'm horrified to see them both nibbling away so blatantly for all to see. Princess is quickly dissecting a raspberry filled turnover, and it looks as if a massacre is taking place in front of me.

A thin redheaded girl comes over. Her nametag reads *Bailey*, assuring me she's the girl I met the night of the murders.

"Can I help you?" A brief smile stretches across her face.

"Hi, Bailey, we actually met the other night at the community center in Honey Hollow. Is Crystal in?"

"Oh. No, she's not. She stepped out for a minute." Her demeanor shifts on a dime, and she calls for help from the back as a small crowd walks in. Carlotta heads over to the register and begins ordering what sounds like the entire left side of the refrigerated shelves.

Bailey steps around the counter to talk to me in private. She leans in. "Is there something I can help you with?"

"Actually, yes. It turns out, there was some person or group conning an entire string of bakeries out of hundreds of dollars, and each bakery was hit on the same day, the second of February. Do you think you can check to see if you were hit as well?"

Bailey blinks back. "We weren't short." She shakes her head. "I count out the drawers every night myself, and I happen to know I was working that day because the second is Crystal's birthday. She has the whole day off. I closed the shop that night."

"I guess you would know then." Sounds like a dead end. But—while I have her attention. "Bailey, did you notice anything strange afoot the night of the murders?"

She shivers at the mention of it and warms her arms with her hands.

"You know, I didn't say this to that detective woman who came snooping around, but I guess I don't mind telling you." She steps in close and my mouth falls open because I happen to know she's referencing Ivy Fairbanks, Noah's partner.

"What is it?"

Both Princess and Taffy zoom over as if they were magnetized to the impending confession.

Bailey glances to the door. "That woman who was coordinating the event? Larissa Miller?"

"Yes?" I nod, waiting with bated breath at what she might reveal.

"I ran into her in the hall behind the kitchen, and I heard her telling someone that she needed to get paid. It sounded like she was shaking them down. Something about making sure they made the payment on time. She was frantic. Her whole body was shaking. I've never seen anything like it. It was strange."

"That does sound strange." *She* needed to get paid? I thought she owed people money. Huh. Probably both.

"Anyway"—Bailey shrugs—"sorry that your bakery was hit. I'll double-check with our accountant. I'm pretty good at counting the drawers, but he's meticulous when it comes to our finances. Nobody cares about this place like Ian—except maybe Crystal." She shrugs. "Between you and me, she's got a bit of an ego." Bailey heads back behind the counter just as a blonde bombshell encrusted in rhinestones breezes in as subtle as a hurricane.

Crystal shoots a glance my way before doing a double take at the bakery shelf Princess and Taffy all but decimated.

"What in tarnation is happening with my baked goods?" Crystal shrieks and grips her cotton candy-like hair while having a genuine freak-out over the raspberry carnage that's taken place. "Lottie Lemon! Are you responsible for this?"

Carlotta speeds over and grabs me by the arm. "This is our cue to skedaddle."

And skedaddle we do.

All the way back to Honey Hollow.

But I can't get my mind off the fact something has Larissa Miller running scared like a little girl. Who could she possibly owe money to and for what? Better yet, who owes her money?

And Ian's name came up again. He does the books for Crystal's bakery, too. Interesting.

No sooner do I get back to my own bakery than I notice I've a missed call from both Jodie and Ruthie. It turns out, both bakeries were short two hundred dollars that day.

Two hundred dollars? I bet that's what Larissa was shaking them down for.

But why?

13

The best part about ending a long day at work is being able to come home to my sweet cats, kick off my shoes, and cozy up by the fireplace.

No sooner do I walk through the door to do just that than I spot the flicker of candles. The scent of a pepperoni pizza from Mangias permeates my senses, and Noah Fox stands before me in a flannel and jeans wearing a crooked grin that lets me know he has less than chaste intentions with me.

Princess floats up next to me and gasps. "Would you look at that? It looks as if we're both about to have a romantic evening, Lottie. Now, where are my boys? Everett? Noah?" She zips off to the sofa where Pancake and Waffles are sleeping.

Taffy glides in beside me. "She's renamed the furballs. I'll be asleep in the fireplace. I find a strange comfort among the

flames." He slithers his way into the roaring fire, and I can't help but wince at the sight before reverting my attention right back where it should be.

"Noah Corbin Fox." I take off my coat and I'm about to toss it to the sofa when Carlotta smacks into it and fights her way through my best winter parka as if it were a punching bag.

She emerges the victor as she stomps my coat to the ground before looking at the dining room table.

"Well, lookie here." Carlotta heads over and takes a seat.

"*Sorry,*" I mouth to Noah, and he shrugs it off as if it were no big deal.

We head over to the table and start in on the extra cheese, extra pep feast.

"So, Lot Lot," Carlotta ticks her head my way as she takes another bite—"aren't you gonna tell the hot to trot fox about our covert operation today?"

Noah's eyes widen as he looks my way. "Lottie, tell me you didn't pursue the case further."

Carlotta belts out a laugh. "Have you met her?"

Noah closes his eyes a second too long, and Carlotta rattles off everything that went down this afternoon in

Ashford. She tells him all about Larissa's reported odd behavior, the fact Sweet Sin and Upper Crust were both short two hundred suspicious dollars the very same day Larissa shook them down, and the fact a certain poltergeist infestation turned Crystal's bakery shelves into a raspberry flavored bloodbath.

Noah's dimples invert as he looks my way. "I don't know why none of that surprises me."

A knock erupts at the door and Carlotta bolts up.

"Speaking of surprises, I'm about to knock the socks off both you kids." She makes a mad dash for the door and opens it before pulling in the one person I never thought I'd see in my living room.

"Wiley?" I stand up just as Noah heads over.

"*Dad*? What the hell are you doing here?"

Wiley Fox looks decidedly dapper in an ill-fitted suit, his hair slicked back, and his dimples digging in deep. With the lights dim and the candles flickering, it really does look as if Noah has just duplicated himself in my living room.

"Whoa, whoa, whoa!" Wiley holds his fists up playfully as he pulls his son in for a quick embrace. "I've got an official invite."

"That's right." Carlotta slings her arm around his shoulder. "When Wiley invited me out for drinks, I thought what better place than this one? Lottie's got a kitchen full of liquor just going to waste."

"I don't have any liquor," I say, speeding my way next to Noah. "I don't even think I have wine."

"Sure you do. You've got that fancy Madagascar bourbon, Amaretto, and Grand Marnier."

A dull moan comes from me. "Have you been drinking my baking liqueurs? Carlotta, Madagascar bourbon is code for vanilla."

"Well, *Lottie Da*," Carlotta smarts before smacking Wiley on the stomach. "Told you she was a know-it-all."

Wiley gives a wistful shake of the head. "I've got one of those myself," he says, nodding to Noah.

"Nice," I say. "If the two of you are done insulting us, we'd like some privacy now."

"Fine." Carlotta tosses a hand in the air like an ornery teenager. "Can't have the kitchen, then we'll take the bedroom. Come on, Wiley. I've got a stash of tequila in my closet that I've been saving for a snowy day."

Wiley chuckles as he follows along. "Darlin', every day in these parts is a snowy day."

She takes up his hand. "Now you're speaking my language."

Noah and I stare one another down an inordinate amount of time.

"What do we do?" I whisper.

Noah closes his eyes and swallows hard. "They're adults. We ignore it."

"What?"

"Yes." He pulls me in. "This is not how I envisioned this night going." He dots a kiss to my cheek. "This is more like it."

"But the things they could be doing."

"I know." He winces. "But I'm more interested in the things we can be doing." His entire body sags. "Okay, fine. Name what you want me to do to them, and I'll do it."

"I don't know. You pull your weapon and I'll pull mine? Whoever chases them out the door first gets to be the naughty boss for the night?"

A deep laugh trembles in his chest, and just as Noah flinches for his weapon, I stop him cold.

"Wait. You're right. They're adults." I cringe because it doesn't feel one hundred percent accurate. "How about we just continue with whatever else you have planned?" I run my fingers over the stubble on his cheek. "And hopefully, we can both forget the fact my biological mother and your father are getting sloshed in the next room." A thought hits me at a million Miranda Lemon miles an hour. "My mother is going to be devastated if Carlotta uses and abuses your father with tequila."

His brows flex. "On the upside, it does take your mother out of the equation."

I think on it a moment. "Oh, who are we kidding? It was probably destiny. I'm staying out of everyone else's love life."

Noah's lids hood low. "Don't stay out of mine."

"Not on your life."

"How about we kiss and make up?"

I inch back with a laugh in my throat. "We're not fighting, are we?"

"No, but, why deny ourselves the fun part?" Noah finds my lips with his own as he wraps his arms around me. "Besides"—he winces—"there might be something I need to tell you. It's not the greatest news. But it can wait for later."

My stomach knots up because I have a feeling I won't like what he has to say.

"Definitely save it for later."

Noah picks me up and carries me to the bedroom, and I all but barricade the door shut lest Carlotta feels the need to wink-wink sleepwalk her way over while Noah and I are in the middle of apologizing. Noah surprises me with a bubble bath full of rose petals and we cut to the good part right away.

Once we're through, Noah dots a kiss to my cheek as I swim into his lap once again.

"Let's go over the case," I whisper.

Noah's chest rumbles with a laugh and I nearly slip right off.

He pulls back to get a better look at me. "You do realize that crime is my love language."

"Of course." I give his slick chest a light scratch. "Why do you think I brought it up? Let's start with Larissa Miller."

Noah sinks down into the water a notch. "I'm investigating to see if she's been extorting money from people for months."

"What?" My whole body jerks as I struggle to get a better look at him.

Noah nods. "Larissa's been a judge in nineteen culinary competitions since November."

"Nineteen? I didn't even realize there were that many competitions. I must really be out of the loop."

"They're not all for bakers. But after doing a little digging, I think maybe shaking people down for money might be an old song and dance for her."

"Wow. So it begs the question. I wonder how she was going to handle both Whitney and Patricia? That was really brazen of her to take both of their hard-earned money."

"I don't know. Maybe, but it sure upped their odds of winning."

"So would baking a delicious treat. Ugh, the prospect of something as sacred as a baking competition being rigged just boils my blood. Okay, fine, so it's hardly sacred, but dirty money shouldn't be an ingredient in any baking competition."

Noah dots my nose with a kiss. "And I agree. So Larissa might be a crooked judge. But why a double homicide?"

"I guess that way she wouldn't have to disappoint one of them when they didn't come up the victor. Although, that's a pretty weak motive if you ask me."

Noah strokes my hair like strumming a guitar. "I agree."

A thought comes to me, and I twist into him. "Maybe they exchanged notes and threatened to expose her?"

"Now that could be a very strong motive for murder."

"Okay, how about Jodie McCloud?"

Noah blows out a slow breath. "I think something is up with her. Ivy and I went to the bakery, and there was just something off about the way she was behaving. Ivy asked to see the office, and she was slow to comply."

"No offense, but men and women with badges can be intimidating." I think on it for a minute. "I know she wasn't too thrilled that Patricia stole the name for her bakery and then basically hired her to work as a manager. Jodie definitely had a motive. Maybe Whitney was just in the wrong place at the wrong time?"

Noah ticks his head to the side. "But then there's you. Technically, you were in the wrong place at the wrong time, too."

"Agree. What do you have on Ruthie Beasley?"

"She told both Ivy and me she hated the way Whitney treated her. She's still bitter about it. She could have been pushed to the edge."

"Chase Davis?" I ask.

"He could be a wild card. The guy had his ego nicked. But gunning down two women over it doesn't add up."

"That just leaves Ian Gardner and Bailey Wade on my suspect list. What do you have to say about them, Detective?"

"Ian Gardner, the accountant." He gives a wistful shake of the head. "Nice guy. He's attracted to Jodie. We both know that. Closed to new clients until after tax season. That's about all I've got on him." He winces. "Except."

"Except what?"

Noah shakes his head. "It was nothing. It's just when I asked how he knew the victims, he said he hardly knew them at all. Yet, when I reviewed the photos from the photographer that was there the day of the murders, there's a picture of him with his arms around both Whitney and Patricia."

"I saw him do that as soon as I walked into the community center. But maybe he meant it was strictly a working relationship? I'm sure anyone would want to distance themselves from something so horrific."

"You're absolutely right. And I always take that into account. But he did look nervous."

"And Bailey?"

He takes a deep breath, and my own body rises and falls along with him.

"Both Bailey and Crystal Mandrake were characters. Bailey detests the way Crystal treats her. According to the things I heard, it made Whitney sound like a saint. And Crystal—well, let's just say she's her number one priority. She didn't care about the homicides. She did care about beating out the competition."

"There's your killer—and I'm only half-teasing."

"Don't worry, Lot." Noah wraps his arms around my waist. "I'm not taking anyone off the list."

"Are you taking me off the list?" I bite down on a flirtatious smile.

"You"—he plants a heated kiss on my forehead—"are on an entirely different list. A very short list with only one person on it, written right over my heart."

"*Noah.*"

He lands his lips over mine and exemplifies his love for me in the very best way.

In the morning, Noah rises with me early, and we head off to the kitchen to caffeinate ourselves properly, only to find the lights are already on as the sound of murmuring and laughter erupts from the island.

We glance over, and the two of us give a collected groan as I do my best to bury my face in his chest.

"They're not wearing any clothes," I wail. "Is that the bad news you hinted at last night?"

Noah blows out a breath. "No, it's not. But it's pretty darn close."

Noah has bad news for me.

And boy have I ever got bad news for Miranda Lemon.

14

Winter just seems to get colder, longer, and snowier by the day.

The next afternoon, the Cutie Pie Bakery and Cakery is a virtual ghost town—and I mean that literally. It's just Seven—Miles, and a few ghosts haunting the place. And by a few ghosts, I mean Taffy, Princess, and her favorite feline phantom, Thirteen.

Princess and Thirteen have been dating and mating and gorging themselves on a pile of sugar cookies I left for them in my office. Neither Lily nor the kitchen staff goes in there, so it's not a big deal if the stack of sweets slowly dwindles throughout the day.

The bell jingles and I perk up with a smile at the hopes of a real live customer actually crossing my threshold, but it's just Carlotta.

She stalks on over with a hot pink bag from the Scarlet Sage Boutique and pulls out an itty bitty baby blue nightie before plopping it over the counter.

"What do you think?" she barks it out with a laugh.

"I think I won't pass the next health inspection. Would you mind?" I quickly scoop up the trashy negligée and land it back in the bag it came from. "And by the way—you are on full *male restriction*. As in no boys for the duration of your stay at my humble abode."

That wacky grin of hers quickly melts off her face. "What's a matter, Lot? You afraid I'm having more fun than you are? If what they say is true, and the naughty apple doesn't fall far from the tree—you and that naked detective had quite a bit of fun last night."

"Would you keep it down?" I crane my neck past her as that side of beef Everett and Noah paid to stalk me lifts a brow my way. "Carlotta, how could you sleep with Wiley when you know my mother is pulling out all the stops to do the same?" I grimace at the words as they fly out of my mouth. "Not that I'm rooting for her."

"First of all—I didn't sleep with Wiley. Let the record—and the bags under my eyes show that neither one of us got a wink of shut-eye. Secondly—it's not happening again, so you have nothing to worry about. I used up my hall pass. Now Harry and I are even-steven, or should I say *Wiley*."

"Hall pass? You mean what happened between Wiley and you was some sort of revenge sex to even up the score?"

"You're slow, but you're getting there."

"Carlotta, that's terrible. You don't sleep with someone as an act of vengeance. You've got me feeling bad for Wiley and that takes a lot."

"Don't feel too bad for him. He knew what he was getting into. Besides, before he left, I made it clear he needed to hit on your mother like he wants to and stop fearing that wall of youthful muscles that was threatening his very existence."

I make a face. "Noah and Everett simply want what's best for everyone involved."

She waves it off before rattling her bag from the boutique in my face. "This little ditty is going to set Harry and me back on the right track. Oh, and I need to order a dozen or so of those conversation heart cookies with naughty little sayings on them."

"I'm sorry, ma'am. You've got the wrong bakery." I blink a quick smile.

"I'm not here to talk to you. I'm here to talk to Lily." She fishes a twenty-dollar bill out of her purse. "Lily, I've got a tip for you." She takes off for my brunette sidekick, often swayed by the almighty dollar, and now I'm fearing for my bakery's reputation.

The bell on the door chimes and in strides a six-foot-two stack of muscles and legal knowledge—and perhaps the bluest eyes in all of creation.

"Why, Judge Baxter, what brings you to my neck of the woods so early in the afternoon?" I sweeten the words with my cheesiest country accent, and judging by those heavy lids and the twitch of a grin trying to break loose on his face, I do believe he approves.

"What are you up to, Lemon?" He steps up close to the counter and I drink him in with that dark suit and that red satin tie.

"Just standing here contemplating my reputation."

"Reputations are overrated."

"Court end early today?"

"That's right. And I'm not too sorry about it. I miss you."

Every last part of me melts when he says it.

"That tells me we should spend some time together."

"Any word on the case? Have either Noah or you caught a break yet?"

I cock my head to the side. "Have I ever told you how much I love the way you acknowledge my efforts?"

"I might acknowledge them, but they're dangerous and I'm slow to approve."

I make a face. "That's because you have a very real stubborn streak."

His brows bounce. "What you call stubborn others call wisdom."

"Touché."

"So who's the killer?"

"If I knew that, there wouldn't be a case," I say. "Noah and I went over all the suspects last night. Larissa is looking like a strong contender but, in truth, every suspect in this case had a motive." A thought comes to me. "Noah did seem uneasy about Ian. He said he didn't know why. The only time I really spoke to Ian was the night I ran into him and Jodie at Crusty Creations. Maybe it's time I tracked him down again."

"Where's his office?"

"I don't know." I pull out my phone and quickly look him up. "It says here, Ian Gardner, Certified CPA at Infinity Accounting, Hollyhock."

"Wait a minute." Everett leans over and I show him the screen. "Infinity. That's the same CPA firm we use for the lodge. When we bought the place, I just kept the account going."

"Really?" I take a look at the address once again. "Maybe it's time we head over to Hollyhock and see how our investment is doing?"

Everett tips his head back and looks at me through slotted lids. "Only if you let me buy you dinner."

"Deal."

Lily traipses over. "Please tell me you're not taking Miles with you. I feel so much safer with him here, especially now that there's a killer out there targeting bakers." She bats her lashes his way and it takes everything in me not to roll my eyes.

"He's all yours, Lily," I say. "In fact, if it doesn't pick up in the next hour, I say go ahead and close early. Maybe Miles will buy you dinner at Mangias."

"Ooh, I'd like that." She looks his way and he offers her a thumbs-up.

I pack up a box of sweet treats, say a quick goodbye to both her and Carlotta, drop a chocolate fudge brownie off for Seven, or Miles, or Mr. Muscles—whatever he prefers to be called today—and just like that, Everett and I are off to Hollyhock.

15

Hollyhock is all but a whiteout at this snowy hour.

Everett suggested we walk boldly into the Infinity Accounting offices, and that's just what we do. Of course, I brought along a box filled with fresh baked goodies for any and everyone we might encounter. I happen to know firsthand Ian has a sweet tooth—or in the least he has a sweet tooth for a baker named Jodie.

Inside the Infinity Accounting building, it's clean and bright and looks every bit professional. There's a pretty blonde with her hair in a bun and large red-framed glasses seated at the receptionist desk, and we head right for her.

She glances up and quickly does a double take at the handsome man by my side.

"Can I help you?" she practically purrs the words out while looking right at him.

"Yes," I say and it comes out a little snippier than it needed to. "My husband and I were hoping to speak to Ian Gardner about an account we have with him. And I brought a little something for the office." I quickly open the box of goodies and hold it out to her.

"*Ohh,* thank you." She chooses a red velvet cheesecake bite and moans once she pops it into her mouth. "It's so good." She closes her eyes as if lost in its creamy dreamy goodness. "Ian's actually not here at the moment. He's visiting a client. But if it's not one of his private accounts, any of our CPAs could help you with it."

I glance to Everett and give a slight nod.

His chest expands with his next breath. "That would be great."

"Perfect." She leads us up a flight of stairs and we bypass a door with a gold plaque that reads *Ian Gardner, CPA.*

I take up Everett's hand and give it a squeeze, nodding over to the office and he nods right back.

See that? I totally have Everett's permission to snoop to my heart's content. I glance back at the door with a knowing smile just as two supernatural spooks float right out of it. Taffy slithers over and glides over my shoulders, giving me an icy shiver that runs down my spine. Princess doesn't miss a Baxter beat. She quickly hops up and wraps herself around Everett like a white fluffy scarf.

"Finally, darling," she purrs it out seductively. "I get to spend some quality time with the man of my dreams." She whips him in the face with her tail and his lips flicker with a sly grin.

We're brought to a claustrophobic office where we meet with a man named Bartholomew who happens to have a severe dairy and gluten allergy, so my box of sweet treats have been rendered effectively useless. He seems like a sensible man with his plaid jacket, his gold-framed glasses, and not-so subtle comb-over. Certainly he would understand that we're just pretending to be interested in our investment's financial state.

About five minutes into what looks to be a rather exhaustive and extensive dissertation on the shaky state of the lodge, I excuse myself to use the restroom.

"And you know what?" I say, scooping up the box. "I'll take this downstairs and put them on the receptionist's desk. At least that way they'll get eaten while they're still fresh."

Everett's eyes grow large with suspicion. Dear Lord, he didn't really think I wanted to know the great state of financial affairs of the lodge, did he? Okay, so maybe he did. And maybe I should have the slightest interest because I'm knee-deep with a serious mortgage on the place, but that's not the point of this numbers-based meet and greet.

I make wild eyes right back at him and watch as his chest expands as if he were about to blow up to the size of a Macy's Thanksgiving Day float.

"Make it quick, Lemon," he whispers it through the side of his mouth before straightening. "I'd hate for you to miss the recap from the last few months."

Bartholomew shakes his head. "It's not a problem. We can wait for you."

"Oh, please don't. I'm anxious to get to dinner with this guy." I pat Everett on the shoulder as I get up. "He promised me a big, juicy steak. I'm really looking forward to it."

His lids hood as that wicked grin begs to take over. "And I'm looking forward to dessert."

Why do I get the feeling I'm the dessert in question? But then again, Everett is a big, juicy steak of a man.

"Don't be long, Cupcake." He smacks his lips as I hightail it out of there.

Everett sure knows how to pull the husband card when he needs to. Something tells me he doesn't mind one bit.

Taffy hisses as we speed down the hall. "You're going to break into his office, aren't you, Lottie?"

"You bet your sweet spotted skin I am." I give a quick glance around before opening the door to the aforementioned office and sealing myself inside.

It's quiet, eerily so, save for the riotous beating of my heart.

"Figures," Taffy says as he slithers off me and heads for the desk. "When it gets down to the nitty-gritty, the cat is nowhere to be found."

"That's because she's purring soundly over Everett's body. I've taken a nap in that very same spot and, believe me, it's not a place you voluntarily remove yourself from." I land the box of goodies on the desk before heading to the other side and falling into Ian's oversized leather seat. There's a large computer monitor that hums to life once I touch the keyboard and a bevy of files sit right there on the desktop.

"Taffy, look at this," I whisper. "He's got each business in alphabetical order." I quickly scroll down to Sweet Sin. "This is too easy." I open the file and quickly scan it. "He's got it organized by month. Looks like the Sweet Sin is in the money. Not too shabby. I guess all those conversation heart cookies with their poignant sayings are slaying it. No pun intended." I glance down the screen. "What's this?" I point just under the monthly total.

Taffy leans in. "I won't pretend to understand it, Lottie. You tell me what it is."

"It says abatement fee. I wonder what that could be. It sure is significant, at least twenty percent of the monthly total." I scroll down and note the same fee on every month as far back as last year.

"Take a picture," Taffy hisses. "Let's move on. I feel a negative energy about this place."

"Good idea." I quickly snap a few pictures before opening up the Upper Crust file and note the same abatement fee. I open up a few other files for a few more bakeries, including A Cake Above and note the same terminology, at about the same percentage. "Maybe that's his fee?" I say to myself as I scan the file. "But up here it says Infinity monthly billing. *Huh*."

The door rattles and starts to open and I quickly dive underneath the desk.

"Lemon?"

A wave of relief washes over me as I take a moment to catch my breath.

I crawl out from underneath the wooden structure and click out of the file I left open.

Everett takes me by the hand and leads me right out of the office as if the building were on fire.

"Everett, I left my—"

He pulls me into a darkened corridor just as a couple of men head this way, and he crashes his mouth to mine. Everett secures his hands over my cheeks and holds me there while moving his lips against mine as if he were a man on a sultry mission.

Princess purrs so loud it sounds as if a helicopter were about to land on our heads.

"Oh, Lottie, you really are the luckiest girl in the world. First a bath with Noah, and now office kisses with Everett?"

Everett pulls back and frowns at that bath comment, and I give a little shrug.

Footsteps quicken in our direction, and he lands his kisser right back where it belongs and my stomach does that roller coaster thing it's accustomed to with one of Everett's steamy kisses. For some reason, this one feels like the steamiest kiss of them all.

"It's just a couple of overheated accountants," a man's voice strums out and the sound of another one chuckling at his comment accompanies it. "Probably looking for a room to duck into. Trust me, Ian. No one was breaking into your office."

I gasp up at Everett, and he nods.

"Well, look at this?" a voice that sounds decidedly like Ian's belts out. "It looks as if someone did break into my office." Horror of all horrors! "My girlfriend must have dropped by. She left a box of cookies. And they say true love is dead."

I press my fingers to my lips. Am I ever glad I didn't seal the box with a sticker that bears my bakery's cheery moniker over it.

Ian moans with delight.

Another chuckle comes from the other gentleman. "Cookies at the office? You got a keeper there."

"I've got trouble is what I got," he teases. "But like I've always said, I'd do anything for her. She's the reason I'm headed to that bake-off this Friday."

I offer Everett a crooked grin. That's exactly where I'll be.

Princess gasps, "That's your bake-off, Lottie! You're going to win. I just—"

"Would you hiss up?" Taffy ironically *hisses* so loud it cuts right through my eardrum.

"Bake-off, huh?" the other man says. "Hey, did you hear about those killings? Two bakers shot dead right there in Honey Hollow."

A moment of silence bounces by and Everett and I exchange a look.

Ian sighs. "That's Honey Hollow for you. Murder capital of the world, it seems."

I make a face because he happens to be right.

"Sounds scary," the other man points out. "If my girlfriend was a baker, I'd keep tabs on her."

Everett caresses my cheek with his thumb, and I'm right back to melting again.

"Trust me. Jodie is safe. She's got a concealed weapon with her at all times."

My mouth falls open as I look to Everett.

"As soon as all this trouble started, I made sure she never leaves home without it."

As soon as all this trouble started? As in after the murder?

Their voices and footsteps grow faint as they head in the opposite direction and I blow out a breath I didn't realize I was holding.

Everett and I make a dash for the stairs and head right back out into the falling snow.

We get into the warm shelter of his car and I pull him close by the tie.

"Essex Everett Baxter," I purr out his name and Princess is happy to purr right along with me. "You kissed me." It comes out threadbare as my fingers lose their grip over the silk cloth in my hand.

"It was do or die, Lemon."

A smile crimps my lips. "It was life, Everett." I give a little shrug.

I can't help but wonder if what my grandma Nell alluded to last month was true. She mentioned something to the effect that Noah and I were about to experience one long goodbye. And I hate that it even crossed my mind just now.

"Hey"—Everett reaches over and picks up my hand—"focus on Noah. Focus on the case. Forget about that kiss."

Our eyes lock a moment too long before he finally starts up the car and we head down the road, trying to forget about everything as we lose ourselves in silence.

But I think we both know that kiss was unforgettable.

"Everett? What do you think a monthly abatement fee is, coming from a CPA?"

He shakes his head. "Never heard of it."

"Me either."

I have a feeling that's something I won't be able to forget either.

We grab a quick bite at the Wicked Wok before Everett drops me off at the bakery. No sooner do I get inside and head to my office than I spot another one of those ominous black gift bags.

I dip my hand into it and pull out a necrotic looking cookie, iced in onyx with hot pink writing across it that reads...

Be afraid.

16

Having an overprotective boyfriend can be a bit much. Having two feels as if you're slowly being smothered with love.

Okay, so I'm not being smothered, more like safeguarded. Suffice it to say, Noah and Everett lost their cool as soon as they heard about it. Lily is the one that actually put the bag on my desk. She said she found it on the table nearest the door and said that it had my name on the tiny tag attached to it.

Noah and Everett reviewed the security footage with me, and from what we could tell, whoever it was, they managed to conceal themselves in a huge crowd that was sent over as a part of my mother's The Last Thing They Ate Tour.

Speaking of Miranda Lemon, it's the very next night and she's hosting her couples' truth or dare affair, which evidently consists of a large social mixer in which you're supposed to play a little game of truth or dare before you can carry out a conversation. There are plenty of people crammed into the conservatory, and everyone looks single and ready to mingle—and perhaps slightly sloshed, no thanks to the wily bartender my mother procured.

And since I'm here catering the event, Noah, Everett, and our silent but deadly friend Seven is here as well. Even though he crumbled like a cookie and spilled his real name to Lily, I still don't feel comfortable referencing him by his formal moniker.

The conservatory is already booming with bodies and loud boisterous music as I put out my last party platter filled with decorative sprinkle cookies, brown sugar cookies filled with caramel and peanut butter, toasted pecan snickerdoodles, hazelnut mini muffins, rocky road brownies, French vanilla cookie bars, red velvet cheesecake cookies, miniature powdered donuts, chocolate iced mini donuts as well as a bevy of red velvet cupcakes.

My mother wanted a delicious variety, and a delicious variety she got.

A familiar looking spook floats up this way.

"Boo." He grins as he says it and licks his lips at the sugary fare before him. Winslow Decker is a handsome man—albeit dead—who Greer Giles snapped up as soon as she got to the other side. "It all looks great, Lottie. And thank you for the treats you left in the pantry. Greer and Lea are there now enjoying every last bit. Which brings me to my next point. Greer's first death day is this Saturday. Would you bake the cake?"

A mean shiver rides through me as he says it. "Must you call it a death day? That does sound rather grizzly." I bob my head to the music so that to the average person it looks as if I'm singing along.

Thirteen pops up between us on the table that has all of my sweet treats laid out.

"Grizzly it's not." His black fur sparkles as if he were covered with glitter. "Oh, just wait until you're dead, Lottie. The wonders, the anti-gravity, the all-you-can-eat buffet at the Cutie Pie Bakery and Cakery—after hours, of course."

My mouth falls open, and I laugh at the thought.

I turn to Winslow. "Of course, I'll bake a cake. Any idea of what she might like?"

Winslow lifts an illuminated finger. "I was thinking about a three-tiered wonder covered with those conversation heart cookies with the words *Winslow loves Greer*."

Thirteen twitches his whiskers. "And add *Thirteen loves Greer*. As obnoxious as that beauty queen can be, she's *my* obnoxious beauty queen."

"Add my name, too," a curt little voice erupts from behind and I find Lea holding up her machete at me in a threatening manner. "Where's that pink slimy snake? I want to chop off his tail."

I make a face at the growing crowd. "Most likely with Carlotta. They've been chummy-chummy for the last two weeks. I think they see a lot of the same qualities in one another. And I'm not even sure that's an insult."

Thirteen growls, "Warn me when the ball of fluff arrives."

I can't help but grimace. "Has she worn out her welcome?"

Thirteen's lips look as if they're curving to the ceiling. "The only thing that sweet kitten is wearing out is me."

"Lottie?" a shrill female voice calls from behind and I turn to see my mother waving wildly at me so I head on over. "Lottie, please don't stand alone and mumble to yourself. People are going to wonder."

"But I was singing." I shake my head because, face it, Miranda Lemon knows me well enough to see through a musical half-truth.

"Never mind that." She spins me around. "You shouldn't be talking to yourself. You should be talking to those boys." My eye hooks to Everett and Noah who are currently being accosted by my least favorite residents of the B&B, Cressida and Cormack. "Lottie, you can't leave two handsome men like that alone. They're liable to catch a floozy." She chortles at her own slight as she shoves me off in their direction.

I'll admit, those floozies look as if they're getting awfully cozy with my two favorite men. Cormack is wearing a pink velvet gown with a plunging neckline, and Cressida looks like a glass of champagne personified in an off-white glittering number. Both women look as if they should be at some fancy cotillion and not at my mother's mostly senior V-Day bash.

Cormack lifts a cherry red cocktail my way before leaning against Noah's chest. "Did you tell Layla the news?"

I avert my eyes. There is no end to Cormack's gloating behavior.

I pull Noah over by way of his tie. "If by news, you mean the bad news he's been meaning to share—we're putting it off." I lean toward Cressida who's doing her best to stick her tongue in Everett's ear. "And you're just bad news altogether."

She snorts as she lifts her drink my way. "Be gone, Leah. These men don't belong to you anymore."

"Good Lord," I say as I look to Noah. "What's your father putting in those drinks, anyway?"

Noah's dimples dig in deep and I'm tempted to land a kiss into each one of them. "It's called Love Potion Number 9. He says the recipe belongs to his apprentice for the evening." He nods to the bar, and I look over to find a cackling witch by his side, a stunning yet wicked Serena Digby.

My mouth falls open. "Do me a favor and don't drink anything tonight unless it comes in a sealed container."

"Too late." Cormack flicks my nose. "Cressie and I have been steadily imbibing ever since we got here."

"I'm pretty sure that's not how it works." I make a face at Everett for letting the blonde bimbo suction herself onto him.

"Lemon. Truth or dare."

"Dare," I say, looking right at the handsome judge. "I dare you to lose the blonde accessory."

Everett glides forward and lands by my side. "Your wish is my command."

Cressida rolls her eyes. "Truth or dare, Essex."

"Truth." His lips cinch on one side.

Cressida slinks over, her chin pointed down, her eyes looking up at Everett as if she were doing her best to cast a spell.

Figures. Serena really is a wicked influence on these two featherheads.

Cressida takes a breath, expanding her bosom all the more. "You're looking forward to our upcoming getaway."

She says it like a command and I inch back in disbelief. Everett wouldn't go anywhere with Cressida. She's a bona fide psychotic.

Everett's mouth opens as he glances my way and he all but winces. "I am looking forward to the trip."

Now it's my mouth falling open.

Cormack hops up and down and cheers. "Go ahead, Noah. Tell Lee-Lee our big news."

"Noah?" I blink over at him as I brace myself for whatever this might be.

Noah exhales hard as he shoots a quick glance to Everett. "I'm actually going on this trip as well."

"What?" A laugh bubbles right out of me. "When and where? What exactly is going on?"

Noah winces as if it pained him to extrapolate.

"Truth, Noah," I say. "I *dare* you to tell me the truth."

Noah's lips part and he quickly closes them again.

"Everett and I are going on a guys' weekend." He shrugs and I can tell he's stretching the truth. "Cormack and Cressida just so happen to be headed in the same direction."

Now it's my mouth opening and yet not a sound comes out.

"Lemon." Everett shakes his head. "Don't overthink this."

"Did you say weekend?" I turn back to Noah. "As in *this* weekend? Valentine's Day weekend?" A choking sound comes from my throat because I can't seem to get another word out. But the silence emitting from Noah and Everett is saying far more than words could ever hope to convey. "Excuse me. I think maybe I do need a drink."

I quickly thread my way through the crowd and head for the bar.

Wiley is busy chatting up my mother—my poor mother, whom I don't have the guts to tell the awful truth to about him and Carlotta and the indecent things they were most likely doing in my innocent spare bedroom.

Serena floats my way as smooth as an apparition as if she were meeting me halfway.

"How's it going?" Her left brow hitches into her forehead like a fishhook. "Have they dumped you yet?" She cranes her neck past me.

"If by *they* you mean Noah and Everett, then yes. They've dumped me." I shake my head while snapping up one of the fruity drinks on the tray before me. "How did that hex you placed on me go again? Ashes to ashes, dust to rust? Oh, that's right. I don't believe in curses."

Her cherry-stained lips purse to the side. "You will." She snickers to herself as if it were hilarious. "But if you need a refresher on what was said, I believe it went something like—you will rue the day you trampled on the hearts of those girls. Everything you love, everything you desire, everything you hope for and dream of, will turn to ashes and soot." She lifts a finger and glances to the ceiling as if straining to recall the rest. "May nothing go your way. May the shadow replace the sun. May the winds of fortune hide their face from you. May darkness descend on you this hour, and may it never leave until you surrender all that you stole from my sisters." She smears a dark smile across her face. "Word to the wise— let go of Noah and Everett. It's clear you can't decide which one you want for yourself and it's bad form to keep both. Why don't you let them be for a while? Who knows? The distance might offer clarity. But then, by the time you decide it will be too late." She nods just past me. "Some might say it's already too late."

I glance back, only to find Noah and Everett indulging Cormack and Cressida in what looks to be a genuine conversation. It looks sane, intimate, and the four of them very much look like couples.

"It can't be true," I say, taking a few steps forward. "I can't be losing Noah and Everett."

Noah wraps an arm around Cormack's shoulder as he leans in and says something to their tightknit circle and the four of them nod in unison.

They're probably agreeing on what a fool I've been.

Carlotta comes up and swats me on the back as if she were killing a housefly.

"What's up, Lot? You look like you just saw a ghost. Scratch that. You look far more like yourself when you're gawking at a supernatural spectacle. Is this because Lea chopped Taffy up into bits and pieces? I wouldn't give it a second thought. Winslow is working him together like a jigsaw puzzle."

"No. It's because nothing seems to be going my way as of late."

"Sorry about that. The good news is, with your surplus of hot hunks, you're still liable to get lucky tonight."

"I don't know. It looks as if I might be down two good men."

Carlotta follows my gaze and clucks her tongue. "That's rough. Losing two men in one night? Maybe you're cursed, kid."

I glance back to Serena and she gives a sly wink.

"Maybe I am."

17

"Bear!" I marvel at the newly renovated community center as I take a quick survey of the place. "I can't believe you did all this in under a month!" Bear is turning into Honey Hollow's premier contractor.

"It was easy, Lot. I wasn't moving walls or anything. I just put in new flooring, painted, installed new kitchen appliances, and redid the island and counters. Did a little overhaul to the restrooms. Easiest money I've made in a long time."

"Well, it looks fantastic," I say, marveling at the rustic wood flooring. Gone is the deep navy wall color, replaced with bright white, which really opens up the place ten times more than before.

Multiple makeshift kitchens dot the cavernous interior, and just beyond that, a set of grandstands are set up for anyone who would like to watch the competition live and in person. There are portable ovens, refrigerators, and several stainless steel work surfaces to accommodate all twenty-two bakeries that are participating in today's festivities. The crowds have already filtered into the building and the grandstands are nearly filled to capacity. Vermont's public cable television is filming the event for its scheduled programming slot next week.

The thought of being on TV in any capacity is more than nerve-wracking. Lily has been green all morning—so has Keelie, but for entirely different reasons. Both Lily and Keelie are working as my sous chefs. Even though baking isn't necessarily Lily's forte, she begged for the chance to be on TV and I didn't have the heart to crush her Hollywood dreams.

Lily and Keelie wave us over.

"*Lottie.*" Lily looks frazzled and we haven't even begun the competition yet. "Please tell me we have enough ingredients for everything you plan on baking. It's too late to put in an order for more ingredients. Do you understand me? It's too late!"

Keelie rolls her eyes. "Lily, stop freaking out. Lottie is a pro." She shoots those baby blues my way. "Tell me you have enough ingredients, Lottie Kenzie Lemon, or I will flip a table."

Bear and I share a laugh at their expense.

But Bear's demeanor changes on a dime. "You do understand you have the home turf advantage, Lot. Missing an ingredient would be a sophomoric blunder."

I avert my gaze. "Do not worry about ingredients." I'm far more worried about the fact it's Friday the thirteenth, but I don't dare breathe a word. I'm not exactly a horseshoe of a person—I'm more of a walking, talking broken mirror. "The competition has a stocked pantry that's available for use to any of the contestants. And the items I brought along have already been approved for use by the judging panel." Speaking of which...

I glance over to the elongated table situated in front of the baking area. Several men and women mingle with one another, all looking rather conservative but friendly in general. I spot Larissa Miller speaking with Bailey Wade from A Cake Above Bakery, and I can't help but wonder if Crystal is having her lackey grease the judge's palm.

"Excuse me," I say as I head that way, but before I can make my way over, I'm waylaid by my sisters, both looking mildly panicked for me. I'm sensing a theme.

"Lottie"—Lainey grips me by the fingers—"tell me you've got your best recipes on hand. The competition looks really stiff."

"Believe me," I say. "I've brought all the firepower I've got." Sans Ethel, of course. I realize that Noah and Everett want me to bring my gun wherever I go, but seeing that both

Noah and Everett will be here, I didn't see the point. "And by the way, you look adorable." I pull back to admire her tiny baby pooch finally starting to appear without a doubt.

"Are you kidding? My jeans are buttoned together with a rubber band, and I'm wearing the biggest sweatshirt I could find. Mom said she'd take me maternity shopping. Hey, you guys should come, too. I figure we'll be sharing a maternity wardrobe anyway. We should pick out the clothes together."

Meg grunts. Her hair looks freshly dyed black, and I can see a purple rim along her forehead, clueing me in on the fact she did it herself.

"I'll go," Meg says. "But when I'm knocked up, I'm still wearing skintight clothes. I don't want to look like a walking circus tent."

"I'm all for tents, Lainey," I'm quick to counter. "I'm all about comfort. I figure when Everett and I are ready to have a baby, he won't mind if I'm walking around in muumuus for a couple of months. Heck, I'll probably live in them after that, too. I like swimming in my clothes."

Both Lainey and Meg look at me as if I've sprouted another head.

Lainey wrinkles her nose. "I thought you and Noah were on-again."

Meg shakes her head. "Are you off-again?"

"No, we're on-again. And things are working beautifully." Or at least they were until Serena Digby's hex reared its ugly head.

Lainey shrugs. "But you said Everett's name. You said, when you and *Everett* are ready to have a baby."

I blink back. "Did not."

Meg barks out a laugh. "You sure did, Lot. I think we know who's stolen your heart."

"That's not true. They've both stolen my heart." I bite down on my lip as I crane my neck through the crowd. "Look, my nerves are frazzled. I hardly know my own name. If I end up with flour on my face or a spatula in my hair, give me a hand signal or something." I spot Chase Davis talking to Everett near the grandstands. It looks as if they've both just arrived. So strange that Chase would want to be here. "I'll be right back."

It takes a bit of effort to navigate the crowd, but I finally appear before them and my heart detonates as I pull Everett into a firm embrace. He's dressed down from his usual power suit but still looks stunning in a black coat and corduroys. Having a baby with Everett would be magical. I know he would be a wonderful father.

Everett cares for those he loves with an aggressive fierceness. But then, so does Noah. If I could only figure out how to mash them into one person, that would make things a heck of a lot easier.

Chase grins over at me. "Mrs. Baxter." He laughs as he shakes my hand. He's casually dressed in jeans and a flannel, and his blond hair is slightly mused. "Still can't get over the fact someone finally pinned this one down."

"It wasn't easy, but someone had to do it," I tease while wrapping my arms around the wall of beef beside me. I'll admit, it's fun to go along with our matrimonial madness. "So what brings you here?"

Chase shrugs. "It's Whitney's last hurrah. I'm not sure what her mother is going to do with the business, but the rest of the employees are here in Whitney's name. No offense, but I'm rooting for the Upper Crust."

"None taken," I say. "I think it's kind of them. And I'm sure she'd appreciate your support."

"Maybe she would, maybe she wouldn't. She didn't think too much of me to begin with, as evidenced by the no-show at our wedding. Do you know people have actually accused me of doing the deed? Like I would ever gun down two women. I've got a great plan for my life, and prison isn't on it."

Everett slaps his old friend on the back. "You're a good guy. I'd like to think Whit is smiling down on you."

Chase excuses himself and takes a seat up front.

"So, Lemon, are you ready to take this thing all the way?"

I can't help but shoot him a curt look. I'm still not sure why he and Noah are being so secretive—and involving themselves with Cressida and Cormack of all people.

"I'm ready to take this all the way." A soft smile presses from me.

"How about a kiss for good luck?" he offers.

"Yes, please."

Everett dots my cheek before heading to the grandstands himself.

I spot Ian Gardner and Jodie a few feet away and my heart strums wildly. I still haven't recovered from that close call at his office the other day. And I certainly haven't recovered from that steamy kiss Everett dished out while we were there.

I put it out of my mind as I head over to say hello.

"Ian, Jodie! So great to see you both. Isn't this exciting?"

Jodie laughs and her ponytail whips back and forth. "If you run off adrenaline, it is. I'm a bit more low-key by nature, so I brought my emotional support boyfriend," she teases as she pulls him in.

Ian chuckles. "I suspected you were using me for some time." He gives a playful wink.

My mouth opens then closes. Instead of offering a glib quip, I decide to see if I can juice the moment for all its worth.

"Don't feel bad, Ian." I manufacture a smile. "I brought two of my emotional support boyfriends." I turn to Jodie. "Lord knows you've got to milk them for all they're willing to give you."

She barks out a laugh. "Why do you think I keep this one around?"

A crowd bustles between us and Ian quickly shuttles Jodie to her station.

I turn just as Taffy and Princess materialize by my side.

Taffy slithers over my shoulders and I'm actually beginning to appreciate how calming the feel of his heft is. Princess glows like a star as tiny sparkles emit from her fur every now and again, reminiscent of her steady Eddie, Thirteen.

"Hey?" I whisper. "You're glowing more than usual. What's your secret?"

Taffy hisses in my ear, "She was out frolicking all night with that dark knight of hers."

Princess purrs as she rolls onto her back in midair. "That's right, big boy." She whips Taffy in the face with her tail. Let's just say that furry beast will never, *ever* forget me. Oh, Lottie, I must come back to see him. Nobody strokes my fur quite the way he does. It's darn right criminal to think I might head off to paradise without my lucky number by my side."

"I can't help you there," I whisper. "I can't even help myself here. I have no idea who the killer might be."

A body runs into me and it's Bailey Wade.

"I'm so sorry, Lottie! Crystal has me running back and forth already. I can't wait for this whole nightmare to be over. I'm quitting as soon as the winner is announced. I can't take another minute of her tyranny." She blows out a quick breath. "That felt good to get off my chest." She winces. "You don't think the killer is back, do you? It's kind of creepy to be here again. I thought for sure they would have changed the venue. It's like this whole town is cursed."

"I guess I didn't think of it that way." Partially because Honey Hollow and homicide seem to go hand in hand these days.

Crystal Mandrake strides by in a pair of rhinestone studded heels and a glammed up apron that reads *no room for losers*. Her blonde hair is teased and sprayed, and her lips and eyes look as if they were drawn in by a three-year-old having fun with a fistful of Sharpies.

She stops short and glares at both Bailey and me.

"Hello, Lottie." She digs her hands into her hips before looking to Bailey. "You get yourself back to that station right this minute, young lady. I will not have you cavorting with the enemy." She takes a moment to scowl at me once again. "If you're pumping her for information, you're wasting your time. I don't give my secrets to the help." She speeds off and leaves both Bailey and me with our mouths hanging wide.

Bailey scoffs. "Did she just call me the help?"

"I'm afraid so." I wince. "I'm sorry she treats you so poorly."

"Don't be. I spoke with Ruthie and Jodie. Apparently, it's a running theme." She shrugs over at me. "Lily didn't exactly have nice things to say about you either. Sorry, Lottie." She takes off and both Taffy and Princess chortle themselves into a conniption.

"What are you laughing at?" I hiss. "Everyone knows Lily doesn't have anything nice to say about anyone."

Princess continues to giggle. "It's not true, Lottie. You're a saint compared to some of these catty women." She gasps. "Look to the door. It's that woman—the one that sees the dead."

I turn and spot Larissa talking to Ruthie by the rear exit. Crystal Mandrake might not be easy to work for, but Whitney was a peach herself. Poor Ruthie is so traumatized by her old boss she's getting out of the baking world altogether. She mentioned she'd be going on a cruise soon.

Taffy hisses in my ear, "Lottie, look at their hands."

I glance down and note Larissa taking something from Ruthie and stuffing it into her purse.

A breath hitches in my throat. "She's up to her old tricks again. And she's so brazen. What in the world would drive her to it?"

Taffy groans, "There is no justifying anything with humans. It could be any illicit behavior she's desperate to support. She's wicked. A deviant. And she must be stopped."

Princess tips her head to the side. "I bet she's the kind of woman who keeps a lover on the side."

I shake my head at the thought. "Or it could simply be greed."

I watch as Ruthie makes a beeline for the kitchen, looking visibly upset.

"I'm getting to the bottom of it. I'm not wasting my time with a bake-off that's rigged."

I spot Noah striding in with Detective Ivy Fairbanks by his side and they both look as if they mean business.

I traipse over and quickly grab him by the hand. "Perfect timing," I say, trying to pull him along with me, but he's stalled.

"Lottie Lemon." He reels me in and lands a kiss to my cheek. "You know I'm rooting for you."

"All the rooting in the world won't help me. We've got a cheat of a judge accepting bribes and I want her arrested."

"What?" He looks mildly confused as Ivy folds her arms across her chest. Her hair is slicked back into a glossy bun and her lips are painted a deep shade of crimson. With those large framed glasses she's wearing, she looks every bit like the naughty librarian.

She crimps her lips. "A judge accepting bribes? Sounds to me like someone is laying the groundwork of excuses for why they might lose." She nods to Noah. "I'll go find a seat. And Lottie, I'm here on patrol. There's a very real prospect that the killer might be present. We wanted to keep an eye on things. May the best baker win."

She takes off and I can't help but make a face.

"I'm guessing she doesn't think that's me. But, it doesn't matter, because, like I said, something sinister is afoot. Noah, I just saw Ruthie Beasley give Larissa a wad of cash."

"Here? Are you sure?" He looks just as stunned as I am.

"Yes, it was right over there by the door. Larissa's probably the killer. Whitney and Patricia were probably about to turn her in."

"Ruthie, huh?" Noah glances around. "All right. Here's what we do. Carry on with the competition. Once it's through, if Ruthie is the winner, we'll open a case. I've got this place covered with security cameras. If that exchange happened, believe me, I won't have a problem proving it."

My shoulders sag at the thought of going the long way with this.

"Fine." I hike up on my tiptoes and land a kiss over Noah's lips. "Wish me luck."

His dimples dig in deep as he presses those evergreen eyes into mine.

"You won't need it. You're the best there is, Lottie. You've got it in the bag." He offers another kiss that's far more heated and lingering. "Do your thing, Lot. Have no mercy."

"No mercy," I parrot back as I give him one last embrace before getting to my station. I'm over halfway there when I spot Bailey by the door with Larissa, and I freeze once I see Bailey digging her hand into her purse before handing an envelope to her.

"What in the world?" I say as my feet begin to move in that direction.

"Halt," Taffy shouts while wrapping himself around my waist like a belt. "Stop. Do not pass go. Do not confront a killer without the proper authorities with you. You're liable to get yourself killed."

Princess tips her tiny pink nose in the air and scoffs. "Don't listen to him, Lottie. You don't need a low-lying snake in the grass telling you what to do. We girls can handle a catfight or two. I say, hiss right at her and watch as she scampers away."

Bailey takes off for the kitchen as soon as I arrive, but I block Larissa's path from leaving.

Princess lets out a horrific yowl and does her best to claw Larissa's eyes.

"*Hey!*" Larissa swats at Princess, and I suck in a breath large enough to evict all the oxygen from the room.

"You *can* see the dead!" I all but shout.

Larissa's eyes widen a notch as she freezes solid. "I don't know what you're talking about."

"What were you just swatting at?"

"You," she bleats it in my face, but I don't move. I'm unrelenting in my stance.

Taffy scoffs as if he were bored. "She's lying, Lottie. And I'm betting she's got an aversion to serpentine spirits."

Larissa's eyes grow wide as Taffy darts right for her, wrapping himself around her like a pink polka-dotted scarf.

"Oh my goodness"—her hands fly to her neck—"get this off me."

"I knew it!" I grab ahold of her arm and drag her out the back door just shy of a snow bank. It's so cold outside, I'm already shivering without my jacket. "You're transmundane, aren't you?"

"Oh, who cares." She plucks her arm free from my stronghold and flicks Taffy off herself until he's clear into the parking lot. But that doesn't stop him from slithering right back. "I never wanted anything to do with that supernatural silliness anyway." She hitches a strand of her dark hair behind her ear in haste. "What are you going to do—report me to the sheriff's department?"

"Maybe not for that—but maybe for all the money you've been taking from my fellow bakers. You're accepting bribes. Admit it."

"Bribes?" She inches back as if I had truly caught her off guard.

Princess gets in her face, shaking her hips with a touch of sass. "That's right, missy. We saw the whole thing. And one of Lottie's boyfriends has this place covered with cameras. You've been caught *green* handed."

Taffy juts his head toward her and hisses, "You're a crooked judge, and we bet you're a killer, too."

Larissa balks at the thought, "This is rich." She tosses a hand in the air. "I'm not the killer, Lottie. And I'm not a crooked judge. At least not in the way you're thinking." A depleted sigh strums from her in the form of a paper white plume. "I teach lessons on the side. It's not against the rules, but it could be seen as shrewd. So I do it under the table. Go ahead and report me if you want. I really don't care."

"You teach *lessons*?" I shake my head at her. "On what?"

"On baking. What do you think?"

My mouth falls open.

Princess scoffs. "I don't believe her, Lottie. Tell both of your strong, gorgeous, well-sculpted boyfriends to come out and frisk her—preferably with their coats off. I'd like to see their muscles in action."

I close my eyes an inordinate amount of time.

"You mean you were teaching Patricia and Whitney baking lessons on the side?"

"Yes." She nods. "I was. They came to my place on weekends. I'm teaching several of the girls here, too."

"Ruthie and Bailey." I nod. "But Ruthie isn't even continuing with her baking. Why the need for lessons now?"

"She's not taking lessons now. She took them last month."

"Why not have them pay at your place? Why go around collecting money?"

"Because nobody seems to remember to bring cash with them. That's how I operate. It's an all cash business. Two hundred dollars a lesson. No one ever seems thrilled to pay, either. But they sure seem thrilled to learn all of my best secrets."

Taffy slithers back around my shoulder. "She's telling the truth, Lottie."

Princess gags as she looks to the wily snake. "Well, I don't believe her. Have Noah bring out the handcuffs. I want to see what he can do with them."

Larissa frowns over at the hypersexual kitten.

"Lottie, why are these beasts here?"

"Because there's a killer on the loose in the event you forgot."

Lily pokes her head out the door. "Here you are!" She tiptoes over in an effort not to slip on the snow. "I've got most of the money." She digs a wad of cash out of her purse and hands it to Larissa. "You really did make baking fun." She shrugs over at me. "I want to be able to help you out."

"*Lily*," I balk. "I would have taught you everything I know for free."

Lily wrinkles her nose at me. "What would be the fun in that? I'll see you two inside."

She disappears and I groan.

"Larissa, I'm afraid I owe you an apology." I toss my hands in the air, exasperated. "I guess I thought you were shaking everyone down for money." I examine her for a moment. Larissa is beautiful, smart, and a hell of a baker. "So you don't owe people money? They owe *you* money?" I ask and she nods as if it were a given. "Can I ask why you're in need of so much cash? I mean, I get life is expensive, but you're working two jobs, and it seems as if you're scraping up finances any way you can."

She nods. "The honest way." Her eyes close a moment. "I'm this close to getting together all the funds I'll need to start my own bakery. I'm opening one up in Burlington to be near my family. It's always been a dream of mine, but I didn't want to start off with a ton of debt. Not all of us are lucky enough to have our boyfriends swoop in and do all the heavy financial lifting for us."

"My boyfriends didn't do any of the financial lifting for me," I'm quick to deny it. Although, technically, Noah did gift me a large sum to buy my appliances.

Larissa furrows her brows. "I wasn't talking about you, Lottie. I meant Jodie." Her head ticks back a notch. "And did you say *boyfriends*?"

Princess coos, "Lottie has two of them and they're just the dreamiest you ever did see." She floats down a few notches with a sigh.

Mom pokes her head out the door. "Lottie? There you are! Would you ladies get in here? Their miking up the contestants. Oh, this is so exciting, Lottie! You're going to be a star. I just know it. And by the way—Wiley is here as my guest. It's our official first date. We're finally getting somewhere!"

Nowhere Carlotta hasn't already been, I say to myself just as she ducks back inside.

Larissa takes a step and I block her path once again.

I squint over at her. "What did you mean by Jodie is opening a bakery?"

"Ask her yourself. We've got to hustle." She goes to take off then takes a quick step back. "Oh, and Lottie? There's a reason I never approached you about my services. You really are the cream of the crop. There's no improving on perfection."

A tiny smile breaks free. "Thank you, Larissa. I appreciate that."

Inside, we're quickly shuttled to a staging area where they strap microphones onto our bodies and go over a few basics as far as how we present in front of the camera. Both Lily and Keelie are shaking like a leaf, but my attention keeps wandering to Jodie.

Soon enough, the cameras are rolling and we're in the throes of mixing ingredients, tugging at unfamiliar appliances, and trying to figure out how to survive in the utter chaos of it all. There are three mandatory desserts, which consist of cookies, pie, and cake, and I've already got the cookies in the oven and the pie ready to go in as well. I'm making my well-loved rocky road chocolate chip cookies, a salted caramel version of my famed cutie pies—the namesake of my bakery—and a red velvet three-tiered cake that I plan on festooning with my iced conversation heart sugar cookies. The exact cake that I'll be giving to Greer tomorrow night for her very first death day.

At about the halfway point, production stops for a fifteen-minute break and we're all unhooked from our microphones long enough to use the restroom or grab a cup of coffee.

Everett waves over at me, and I wave back. He's seated next to Cressida, and it takes everything in me not to scowl at the sight. Of course, she's here. She's always here. I glance to the other side of the grandstands and spot Noah with Cormack by his side. And there's that.

Lily and Keelie take off for the restroom, and I spot Jodie heading for the kitchen so I quickly follow along.

Jodie glances back as we head into the area teaming with the production crew enjoying takeout from the Wicked Wok.

"Hey, Lottie." Jodie laughs. "Was that insane or what?"

"It's just like another day at the bakery—on steroids."

"You got that right." She wipes the sweat from her brow.

"I hear congratulations are in order. Larissa mentioned you were opening a bakery."

Her lips part as she glances to the crowd just past me. "I am."

"I guess you won't be needing that job at the lodge after all. You must have gotten a loan pretty quickly. I mean, it was just a couple of days since we last spoke about it."

Her eyes steady over mine. "Just between you and me, I didn't get a loan. Nobody would give me one on my salary. Let's just say I did someone a huge favor and they owed me. Eventually, it would have happened anyway—but things moved along a lot quicker." She shakes her head as she glances to the door once again. "I think I'm going to grab some fresh air." She stalks off and I'm left trying to decipher her cryptic words.

Jodie did someone a huge favor.

My heart thumps wildly at that prospect.

Could that favor have involved murder?

18

An icy breeze pushes through, blowing the fresh snowfall off the evergreens and sending it sifting slowly to the ground.

The parking lot is filled to the brim, and I spot Jodie leaning against the trunk of a beat-up Toyota.

Without hesitation I speed that way.

Taffy slithers down my body, cinching himself around my legs as if trying to constrict my movements.

"I'm rather against this, Lottie," he hisses. "Isn't this the same spot my Patricia lost her life?"

Princess gasps. "Oh no, I won't go a step farther, Lottie. This is where my Whitney breathed her last. This isn't right. You can't make me."

"You can go back in," I whisper. "This will just take a second."

"You don't have to tell me twice." Princess scampers off, inspiring Taffy to slither back up over my shoulders.

"And then there were two. Try not to get yourself killed, Lottie. I wasn't exactly a big help with the last homicide that took place out here."

I offer him a wry smile as I come upon her.

"Jodie? Everything okay?"

Her tiny ponytail flicks in the air as she straightens at the sight of me.

"Lottie?" She shakes her head as she wipes down her face. "I'm fine. The stress was getting to me, that's all."

The closer I get, the easier it is to see the crimson tracks in her eyes.

"Jodie, you're upset. Are you sure everything is okay?"

She rubs her arms with her hands in an effort to warm herself. But adrenaline is surging through me, making my blood boil without meaning to. It doesn't seem to matter that we're standing in what could easily qualify as permafrost. I don't feel a thing.

"Everything is not okay." Her chest bucks with emotion. "Everything is the opposite of okay." She offers a short-lived smile through tears. "Life just isn't what I thought it would be." She shrugs as she gives a hard sniff.

"Does this have anything to do with Ian?"

Her eyes flash like lightning as she looks my way. "I wish I never met him."

"I'm so sorry, Jodie. This has got to be a tough day to deal with any grief a relationship might bring." I take a bold step forward. "Jodie, Ian does the books for Sweet Sin, right? Have you ever looked at the books before?"

Her eyes widen to the size of my now infamous sugar cookies.

"You know, don't you?" She gives a slight nod, and my mind swirls with the possibilities. That abatement fee comes back to me.

"Oh my goodness." My fingers fly to my lips. "Ian was skimming off the top, wasn't he?"

Jodie gasps, her eyes locking to mine with horror. And I don't need her to say another word to confirm it.

Taffy snaps and hisses as he rouses to life, "Shall I offer her a firm embrace, Lottie? You know I've been craving a good constriction. Don't deny me now."

I shake my head at him just barely, my gaze never leaving hers.

Another thought comes to me. A far more sinister one.

"Ian was stealing," I say. "That's why you didn't need a loan, isn't it, Jodie? And that huge favor you did—" I can hardly catch my next breath at the thought.

Her car chirps to life. "It's not true." She shakes her head. "I can prove it to you." She opens the rear door on the passenger side and I follow her over as she plucks a slender steel gun out from under the seat and points it right at me.

Oh no.

A dull laugh pumps from her. "You're not the brightest bulb, are you?" She hitches her head toward the woods. "It looks as if that famed killer is about to strike again. It's a terrible time to be a baker, isn't it, Lottie?"

My hands slowly rise above my shoulders. "It doesn't have to be this way, Jodie."

"It's too late," she huffs it out, incredulous. "Of course, it didn't have to be this way. If Patricia and Whitney hadn't exchanged notes. They dragged Ian out here to confront him. He wanted to leave the country. But I pulled a gun on them— this gun. My gun, Lottie. I heard Honey Hollow wasn't safe. I brought it with me that night."

"Your gun? Ian didn't shoot them," I say. "He couldn't do it. Could he?"

Taffy growls, "Let me at her, Lottie. I've got a bone-crushing embrace I'm hungry to dole out."

"No." A dark laugh expels from her, and for a second I think she's answering the serpentine specter among us. "I knew Patricia and Whitney weren't going to stop until Ian was put away. And if they ever traced those funds, I wouldn't be looking so innocent either. Ian was taking care of me. He took care of *us*. We had a good thing. My bakery was coming down the pike. It just arrived a little sooner than anticipated, no thanks to their snooping."

"Jodie, Ian was stealing from them. He was probably stealing from all of his clients." I glance behind me and spot an errant branch the size of a baseball bat. "They had every right to be upset."

The sound of the large steel door to the community center shutting blasts through the air. And while Jodie cranes her neck in that direction, I bend my knees just enough to pick up a branch and hold it behind my right thigh.

She turns back abruptly and steadies the gun my way at close range.

"And you shot them," I whisper. "Why, Jodie? How could you?"

Another pitiful laugh trembles from her. "Do you think I wanted to? I killed two women in cold blood, Lottie. It was hell. I never wanted to do that. But Patricia laughed and said I would never pull the trigger. That's all she ever did was laugh at me and tell me I couldn't do anything right. Well, I did something right—didn't I, Lottie? And unfortunately for you, I'm going to have to do it again." She shakes her head, incensed. "I knew I should have taken you out that first night. But Ian insisted he take care of you himself by knocking you over the head. All that extra time you had, you can thank him for it. I knew you were more trouble than you were worth."

Taffy strikes at her neck and Jodie flinches as if she could feel it.

"What was that?" she snaps, looking around wildly as if a bug had bitten her.

"A snake," I say as I swing the branch I'm holding and knock the gun right out of her hand and into the snow below.

Both Jodie and I dive for the weapon, and her fingers touch the tip of it as she struggles to wrestle me off of her.

My knee scrapes against the edge of a jagged rock and a howl of pain rips through me.

Jodie reaches back and smashes her palm into my face, doing her best to shove me away. My arm releases from the stranglehold she has over it and I jab her hard in the ribcage with my elbow.

Taffy growls ferociously as if he were ten times his size before he slithers around her chest.

"Say the word, Lottie," he hisses. "I will end her."

Jodie's knee comes up and kicks me in the chin and it feels as if every one of my teeth just shattered.

A percolating anger brews in me like never before and I lunge past her and land on the gun just as her hand slaps over it. She jerks it free, and soon it's pointed right back at me.

"*Word*," I pant, and Taffy laughs a deep, husky growl that sounds more like the threat than anything else.

Taffy's pale body wraps itself around Jodie's chest in one lithe move.

A hard groan expels from her.

Taffy purrs, sounding a lot like Princess, "That's my girl. Just one more minute and you'll join my sweet Patricia."

"Taffy, no," I say just as someone shouts my name from the community center.

Jodie looks that way in a panic. "I'm sorry, Lottie," she says, almost out of breath. "I have to do this."

Taffy cinches around her another notch and a crack emits from her chest right before her arm jerks and the gun goes off as loud as a nuclear detonation.

"*Lottie!*" Noah howls as his footsteps quicken in this direction.

But I don't answer him back. Instead, I swat the gun right out of Jodie's hand and jump on top of her.

"Taffy, *release!*" I thunder. And just like that, the ornery snake slowly floats away, his illuminated being dissipating before my very eyes. "*Taffy!*" I cry out just as Princess sashays her way over.

"Now look what you did," Princess is quick to chastise him as her fur sparkles with the power of a thousand stars. "Lottie, do tell Thirteen I'll move heaven and earth to come back to him." Her pink little nose is the last thing I see. "And kiss those boys of yours for me, would you?"

"Will do!" I call out just as Noah plucks me off the body I'm lying over. He has his gun drawn, the veins bulging in his neck.

"Freeze!" he riots as he spins me out of his arms, and I land right into Everett's firm embrace with the elegance of a dance move.

"Lemon." He buries a heated kiss over my hair. "It's over."

"She did it," I call out to Noah. "She killed Patricia and Whitney. She confessed. And Ian"—I turn to Everett—"Ian's been stealing from his clients for months. Abatement was code for taking what's not mine."

Ivy runs out with her weapon drawn, and soon the place is crawling with both off and on-duty sheriff's deputies. It turns out, there was more than a handful who came out to watch the bake-off.

"Everett, how did you know where I was?"

"One of the judges said you needed help." He glances to our left and I see Larissa huddled with Ruthie and Bailey.

"Everett, would you excuse me a moment?"

"Sure." He pulls me in tight and I can feel his heart ricocheting against my chest. "I'm not taking my eyes off you." A smile bounces on his lips. "I've been saying that a lot these days."

I shrug up at him. "I'm not complaining."

He takes off toward Noah and Ivy, and I quickly navigate my way to Larissa who excuses herself from the girls she's standing with.

"Thank you," I say as she steps in close.

Larissa folds her arms tightly across her chest. "You're welcome." She nods. "I don't want to be exposed, if you don't mind."

"Of course not." I frown over at her. "Neither do I."

A skeptical laugh brews in her. "Don't you worry, Lottie. I've decided to move to Burlington sooner than later."

"I'd like to keep in touch, if you don't mind. There aren't too many of us in the event you haven't noticed. So, do bad things happen when you see one of those?"

"Ghosts?" A weak smile flexes on her lips. "Yes, but not death. I'm still in the minor leagues, Lottie. I see people trip and fall. Nothing more, nothing less. And I prefer it that way." She inspects me for a moment. "So is your whole family this way?"

"Just my mother—my biological mother. My grandmother was, too, but she's passed."

"My father was. I have an aunt who's transmundane, but her abilities don't include the dead. Have you gone to any of the chapter meetings?" She tilts her head my way as if she were genuinely interested.

"I went to the big convention in New York just last month."

Her mouth falls open. "I was there!" She winces. "Is it odd that I think of you sort of like family now?"

"Not odd at all," I say. "In fact, I'd like to give you a hug for saving my life."

And I do just that.

We wander back inside and the judges eventually agree to carry out the competition.

My cookies were left in the oven a bit too long before either Keelie or Lily noticed them, but my salted caramel cutie pie and three-tiered conversation heart cake turned out spectacularly.

But in the end, Crystal Mandrake took home first place—with me taking second.

I'll take second every time if it means burning my cookies to catch a killer.

You don't get away with murder in Honey Hollow.

Not on my watch.

After a long day at the community center, Lily and I head back to the bakery and relieve the skeleton crew, to close up shop ourselves.

I set the chairs upside down on the tables as I ready to mop the floor and notice a small black bag in the corner.

My heart stops cold.

My fingers tremble as I bring it close. I spot my name printed on the tiny tag attached to the handles before reaching in and pulling out a black iced heart-shaped cookie. And written across the front in hot pink are the words *it's time*.

19

Ian Gardner was arrested and booked for embezzling from his clients. Needless to say, he's no longer with Infinity Accounting.

Jodie McCloud is planning on pleading not guilty to first-degree double homicide. Everett says that she's looking into hiring a team of highly experienced sharks to help get her out of this mess. I can't imagine this will work out in her favor.

It's Saturday. Also known as the most romantic day of the year—Valentine's Day. And since it's one of the busiest days at the bakery, I woke up before the sun ever thought of crossing the horizon and baked myself senseless.

The Cutie Pie Bakery and Cakery had record sales. In fact, we made more than every day this month combined the few hours we were open. I closed a little early since my entire staff wanted to get a head start on the evening.

Naomi had her staff come by this morning and pick up all the desserts for the big dance the Evergreen Manor is hosting tonight.

Noah came home last night—my home—a little after midnight and slept on the couch because he didn't want to wake me. He left for the precinct when I left for the bakery, but he promised me a night I would never forget.

We're meeting at the Evergreen Manor for dinner, along with everyone else in Honey Hollow. And that's exactly where I've just arrived, wearing a gorgeous red dress that shimmers in the light and screams *I love Noah Fox* all over it.

Everett crosses my mind. Of course, I love him, too.

The Evergreen Manor is grand both inside and out. It boasts of white columns that line the front of the giant structure and black iron scrollwork that encases the balconies.

Inside, it's opulent with its dark paneled walls and floors laden with thick emerald carpet. The grand ballroom is cavernous and yet brimming with bodies as every soul in town looks to be present and accounted for—sans Noah, of course. He texted and let me know he's running a touch behind. I told him not to worry about it. When justice calls, I always want Noah to answer. Dinner can wait.

I haul in that three-tiered confection from the bake-off on a trolley myself. I went ahead and adhered dozens of my conversation heart cookies that say *Winslow loves Greer*,

Thirteen loves Greer, Lea loves Greer—I was tempted to add one that read *Greer loves Greer*, but I added something special to that one instead.

Winslow let me know that they would be celebrating this heart-shaped day at the Evergreen with the rest of the town. And it makes sense. Greer seems like a girl who enjoys big parties.

I head down a vacant hall adjacent to the kitchen and a spasm of light twinkles from the seemingly empty break room to my left. But it's not empty at all.

"*Surprise!*" Winslow, Lea, Thirteen, and I cry out as I roll the cake into the room.

The four of them glow a hypnotic shade of purple in the dimly lit room and it's a magical sight to behold. Greer has her hair in wild waves. She's wearing the white ruched dress that she was killed in and has a crystal tiara that sparkles as if it had tiny stars embedded in it pressed over her head.

"Happy death day, Greer," I say, offering my ghostly friend a quick embrace.

She pulls back with tears in her eyes. "You didn't have to do this." Her chest bucks with emotion. "Okay, you did."

The entire lot of us shares a quick laugh, and Winslow leads us into a death day rendition of "Happy Birthday."

Greer gasps as she reads the writing off the cookies one at a time.

"And what's this?" she says, plucking one off near the bottom. "Lottie loves Greer?" She twists her lips. "I love you, too, Lottie."

Greer and I hug it out one more time, and soon enough I leave them to their cake feast as I head back into the ballroom.

"Lemon," a deep voice calls from behind and I spin around, only to find a cutthroat gorgeous man who spikes my body heat without even trying.

"Judge Baxter," I pant. "You look dashing tonight." I frown without meaning to. "And I saw Lily." I shrug. "She's stunning."

"I can't see Lily." He cups the side of my face with his warm hand. "I only see you."

I clasp my hand over his as I bear into Everett's demanding blue eyes.

"You're too good for me," I say.

"No." He shakes his head. "You're too good for me."

Everett and I enjoy dinner with Lily, Lainey, her husband Forest, Meg and her boyfriend Hook, Keelie and Bear—and yes, Naomi and Alex. Dinner comes and goes, and for dessert we're served a slice of red velvet cake with one of my conversation heart cookies set on top.

I haven't told Noah or Everett about my latest dark find. A part of me doesn't even want to think about it on this special day built around love and affection. Besides, I'd like to believe it was from Jodie. She was a baker. She might have thought I was onto her all along.

It could be true. Couldn't it?

Keelie lifts her glass and incites everyone else at the table to do the same.

"I'd like to make a toast," she practically sings the words out.

Naomi groans, "You're supposed to make a toast before you eat, not after. It's the natural order of things."

Keelie smirks at her grumpy sister. "In the event you haven't noticed, I'm not big on the natural order of things." Her free hand pats her belly. "Join me in lifting your glasses to my wonderful, brave, and loyal best friend, Lottie Lemon."

My sisters and everyone else around the table are quick to hoist their stemware into the air.

Keelie wraps an arm around me as she pulls me in close. "I don't know where we'd be without you."

"Probably dead," Meg quips and a warm bout of laughter circles the table.

Keelie howls at the thought, "Here's to not being dead!"

"*Hear, hear*!" those around the table cry in unison.

Lainey leans in. "Can you cool it with the corpses for a few weeks? You've got a birthday coming up next month."

I twitch my nose at the thought. "That I do. But it's no big deal. It's just another day as far as I'm concerned."

My sisters and Keelie exchange a quick glance, and I don't like that plotting look in their eyes.

A bevy of slow songs mewl through the speakers as couples begin to gravitate toward the dance floor.

Everett extends a hand my way. "Shall we?"

My mouth falls open as I look to Lily, and she waves me off.

"My real date just arrived." She all but bares her fangs as she grins at someone just past my shoulder.

Everett and I turn to find a certain single digit monikered man in a black suit with a matching black tie.

"Miles Rock," I say as I shake my head. "Go get him, Lily. He's all yours."

Lily smirks. "That's what I like about him best."

I glance over to Alex who looks as if he just had his ego handed to him by way of a stiletto to the gut. Naomi looks as if she's drooling after the *miles* of muscles as well. A part of me almost feels sorry for Alex. Almost.

Everett takes me by the hand as we weave through the crowd on our way to the dance floor and an eager hand plucks me away from him.

It's Carlotta slow dancing with Mayor Nash.

"Guess who's back together?" This older version of me gives a hard wink.

I nod over at the two of them with a pleasant smile blooming on my lips.

"I'm very glad to see it. I hope no other obstacles stand in the way of your happiness."

Carlotta rolls her eyes and Mayor Nash lets out a hoot.

"She wasn't talking about us, Lottie." Mayor Nash slaps Everett on the back as if trying to coerce him into chuckling along. "Carlotta and I like to mix things up once in a while. This girl is sugar and spice and everything nice, if you know what I mean. I can never get enough of her."

Carlotta honks out a laugh. "More like horns and thorns and everything naughty with a bit of a *bite*." She smacks Mayor Nash on the rear and he riots out a laugh. "I'm also talking about your mama, Lot Lot." She nods just past me where I find Miranda Lemon locking lips with—

"Oh my word. He looks just like Noah from behind." I'm quick to bury my face in Everett's chest, and soon enough he's navigated us deep into the crowd and we're slow dancing, our hearts thumping in time as if they've always beat as one.

"Lemon, I have a favor to ask."

I blink up at the handsome man before me. "Consider it done. And it will be a pleasure."

"Good." He gives a rather short-lived devilish grin. "Don't be angry with me tomorrow."

"What's tomorrow?"

Before he can answer, I'm twirled right out of his presence and into the arms of Noah Corbin Fox. He's donned a dark gray suit, a red silk tie, and he has a naughty twinkle in his eyes that assures me tonight will be a night to remember.

"Holy mother of all things good and right." I swoon at the sight of him. "Has anyone ever told you that you clean up nicely?"

A quiet laugh pumps from him. "You just stole the words right out of my mouth." His dimples dig in with wicked intent. Noah lands a lingering kiss to my lips as he wraps his arms tightly around my waist. "Lottie Lemon, will you be my Valentine?"

A smile warms my lips. "Every single day of the year."

Noah and I dance the night away.

And afterwards we head straight for his place.

He leans in before opening the door. "I thought we might get a little more privacy here than we would across the street."

"I like how you think, Detective."

Noah carries me over the threshold as if I were his bride, and I gasp at the thicket of flora and fauna before us.

"Noah, you must have bought out every florist in Vermont before heading to the Evergreen."

Red roses abound everywhere I look. Rose petals are strewn around the floor and lead in a pathway in front of the fireplace and down the hall.

Toby, Noah's sweet golden retriever, comes bounding out of the bedroom and picks up a single red rose off the floor as he brings it my way.

"Oh my goodness!" I say as I gently pluck the flower from his mouth. "Toby, you have stolen my heart."

Noah gives a playful groan. "You were supposed to make me look good, not upstage me, buddy."

I bite down over my lip as I look to the gorgeous man holding me safely in his arms.

"I think you're better than good, Noah."

He offers a lopsided grin as his gaze grows serious.

"I think we're good together."

And Noah proves it to me, all night long.

In the morning, a perfectly good Sunday, both Noah and Everett pile into Noah's truck and take off like men on a mission—to pick up a couple of blonde bimbos.

Okay, so I don't know if they're actually picking them up and driving to Hollyhock together, but nonetheless I'm speechless.

"Skiing at my very own lodge without me," I balk to Pancake and Waffles. "Can you imagine?"

It's true. In a bizarre turn of events, Noah announced he needed to get going and ushered me across the street to my own home where thankfully there was no sign of Carlotta. She must have spent the night at Mayor Nash's place last night. Something she doesn't make a habit of. But I do appreciate the reprieve.

His ex, Britney, came by as he was leaving and picked up Toby for the day since they still share custody of the adorable pooch.

It's just my cats and me, a roaring fire, and a steaming cup of cocoa. And as relaxing as that sounds, it's not nearly as tranquil as it should be. Especially since I got both Everett and Noah to admit that Cressida and Cormack were somehow weaseling their way to the lodge as well.

Of course, I asked if I could join them and they all but made every excuse in the book. Now it makes perfect sense why Everett asked me to forgive him last night for what he was about to do. He knew he was about to commit the unforgiveable sin—ditching me for a date with a couple of blonde bimbos.

Noah had a hard time looking me in the eye when they left.

As he should have.

"I can't believe they would choose to spend time with Cormack and Cressida. They have to know I'm fuming over this," I say as I pull both Pancake and Waffles in close. "I can't wrap my head around it." I give Waffles a scratch on the head and he rewards me with a commiserating yowl. "None of this seems real. It truly is beginning to feel as if I'm cursed."

A knock erupts at the door and I head over to find an unexpected figure on the other side.

"Oh, it's you," I say. "Can I help you with something?"

"Noah and Everett asked me to give you a ride to the lodge."

"Really?" A thrill sparks through me at the thought.

"Yes, really. Are you coming or not?"

"Give me less than two minutes." I throw a bag together faster than you can shake a whisk, and I hop into the waiting car.

We start in on the drive and we miss the turnout to Hollyhock.

"Hey, I think we missed our exit," I say, glancing back, and something in the back seat catches my eye.

It's an all too familiar little black gift bag, and my heart thumps hard at the sight of it.

Something tells me I'm not going to Hollyhock.

Something tells me this just might be the last ride of my life.

A Note from the Author

Thank you for reading **Sugar Cookie Slaughter (Murder in the Mix 18).**

Look for **Devil's Food Cake Doom (Murder in the Mix 19)** coming up next!

Acknowledgements

Thank YOU so much for spending time in Honey Hollow! I hope you enjoyed this new adventure with Lottie and all of her Honey Hollow peeps as much as I did. The MURDER IN THE MIX mysteries are so very special to me, and I hope they are to you as well. If you'd like to be in the know on upcoming releases, please be sure to follow me at Bookbub and Amazon. Simply click the links on the next page. I am SUPER excited to share the next book with you! So much happens and so much changes. Thank you from the bottom of my heart for taking this wild roller coaster ride with me. I really do love you!

A very big thank you to Kaila Eileen Turingan-Ramos, Kathryn Jacoby and Jodie Tarleton for lending me your eyes.

A special thank you to my sweet betas, Lisa Markson, Ashley Marie Daniels and Margaret Lapointe for taking such good care of the book. And a shout out to Lou Harper for designing the world's best covers.

A hearty thank you to Paige Maroney Smith for being so wonderful.

And last, but never least, thank you to Him who sits on the throne. Worthy is the Lamb! Glory and honor and power are yours. I owe you everything, Jesus.

About the Author

Addison Moore is a **New York Times, USA Today,** and **Wall Street Journal** bestselling author who writes mystery, psychological thrillers and romance. Her work has been featured in **Cosmopolitan** Magazine. Previously she worked as a therapist on a locked psychiatric unit for nearly a decade. She resides on the West Coast with her husband, four wonderful children, and two dogs where she eats too much chocolate and stays up way too late. When she's not writing, she's reading. Addison's Celestra Series has been optioned for film by **20th Century Fox.**

Feel free to visit her at:

Website: www.addisonmoore.com
Facebook: Addison Moore Author
Twitter: @AddisonMoore
Instagram: @AuthorAddisonMoore
http://addisonmoorewrites.blogspot.com